N A T I V E

⅂⅃F

To Sue

thank you
for being you

[signature]

love
Abdul.

NATIVE

ABDUL - AHAD PATEL

NATIVE

Young Adult, Fiction, Fantasy,
Romance, Adventure, Drama

Cover and illustrations by Adam Taie

Images, artwork and poems: Copyright © 2018
Abdul-Ahad Patel

Abdul-Ahad Patel asserts the moral right to be
identified as the author of this work

A catalogue record for this book is available from
the British Library

ISBN: 9781724001726

Abdul-Ahad Patel was born and raised in Hackney, London. He has been a support worker for children with autism, criminal justice substance misuse worker, actor and screenwriter. He has climbed a dormant volcano in Santorini, trains and competes in Brazilian Jiu-Jitsu, and attended high school in Mauritius for two years. He lives in Gloucester and is happily married. Native is his debut novel.

Abdulahadpatel.com

'For the dreamers curious enough to do something unexpected...'

My grandparents and my parents have such beautiful marriages. I don't normally think too deeply about it but I've always been fascinated at how they can embrace one another with so much love and compassion. I guess at eighteen no one can really know what love is.

My artwork is a way of escaping. I like to paint and draw places and people, from my thoughts, creating an image that exists for nobody else but me. Sharing that passion and art is my way of doing that but also of showing where I have escaped to. The only problem is, I haven't shown anyone where I have escaped to...well, not yet. I just don't feel it's the right time yet.

I've never felt as understood as the day you looked into my thoughts and escaped with me, but it was also the day I felt unconditionally about him. My heart locked onto the face of the opposition, but how do I give my mind and heart separately?

NATIVE

TUF

Not many people like the rain, but there is something so beautiful about it. There is the silence and then the tiny thuds it makes when it collides with the ground; the way it stays on the surface of your hand as if it belongs to you. Everything seems more in the moment when it rains. The Prophet Muhammad, in Islam, once said 'Prayers won't be rejected at the time of rain.' Rain is truly a blessing from above, I'm sure going to miss it.

I'm about to dive into the complete unknown and leave home for the very first time, and for somewhere the complete opposite of this rainy town. I'm moving to Southern California to begin my college journey. I am nervous but excited. My parents don't like the fact that I am moving away from home. They'd smothered me all my life and now they had to live with letting their little girl go and grow up.
"Elu…Elu…" my father said to me, as I sat in the backseat of the car and stared at the raindrops on the window. "El, baby, you're going to miss your flight if you keep daydreaming."
      My father squashed his index finger onto the tip of my nose and grinned at me like he had done as far back as I can remember. It was our father-daughter gesture to each other, only he would always catch me off guard.
      "Yeah…yeah, let's, let's go," I said as I detached myself from the beauty of the rain. My mother looked at me with that sense of *don't leave*. My mom and I had a very close bond. She always knew exactly what I was thinking and feeling, but then again I suppose all mothers do.

We walked over to the check-in and boarded my luggage before making our way to the departure zone. I felt so guilty as I knew my parents really didn't want me to go, but they both knew how much it meant to me. I felt sick that the moment was coming when I'd have to say goodbye. My stomach felt as if it was sucking itself in; my throat became dry and felt as if there was a lump in the middle of it; my eyes were bursting to let out tears but I kept sniffing to hold them back, and my hands were so shaky it felt as if the blood was withdrawing from my veins.

"El, you're going to do great and go on to do amazing things. I love you, my angel, and they're going to love you too. Stay safe and call us." My mom trembled with tears as she combed her fingers through my hair in the way she has been doing ever since I was a kid. She then kissed me on the forehead and wrapped her arms under mine. I could feel her tears running down my neck. My body became unstable. I just wanted to fall and cry but I'd never cried in front of my dad. I was daddy's soldier; when he was tough, I was tougher.

"Thanks, Mom. I love you too."

"Rose..." my dad whispered to my mother and she slowly let go, looked me dead in the eyes, and smiled slowly, slipping her hands through mine as if it was the last time we'd ever see each other.

My dad stepped forward to replace my mother. "Ah...growing up fast, ain't ya, kid!" he said as he winked at me. "Elu, my beautiful princess, look after yourself. Make sure you stay safe and stay away from them boys—"

My mother interrupted, "Jacy!"

"It's OK, Mom...Dad!"

"I know, I know. I love you, Elu." My father gripped me tight like never before and right then my tears started to pour out uncontrollably. I tried to speak but the lump in my throat was blocking any sound that wanted to come out. He slowly let go and took one last look at me, half smiled, and squashed my nose. I looked up at my father and he placed both his hands on my face and wiped the tears away with his thumbs. With that half-smile, he looked down at me and whispered out the gap of his mouth, "Go get them, princess."

I didn't say anything; not that I didn't want to, but 'cause I couldn't. I took one step in the other direction and headed past the gates. As I looked back over my shoulder to see my parents see me off, I could see my whole world crumble right before me but a new world built in front of me.

I boarded the plane and sat in my seat next to the window so I could have one more look at home as we left. It was still raining. As the raindrops hit the window I felt a sense of relief. The rain comforted me and kept me calm as I left my old life to start my new one. It was about five hours in all to LAX. I had to stop in San Francisco and switch planes. Grandma used to live in 'San Fran' before she met grandpa back home. Luckily, the seat next to me was empty so I had extra space and more privacy to myself.

During my flight to California, I couldn't sleep or stop thinking about my parents. I was having so many mixed emotions; the freedom of being by myself but also the loneliness of not having my loved ones around me. I needed to escape and keep

my mind occupied for the journey so I took out my
sketchbook. I would just doodle whatever was on
my mind or what could relate to how I was feeling. I
sketched a young Native American boy with a bag
on his back walking away from his tribe; you could
see the tents, the fire, and the mountains in the
background. The boy was in loose clothing, tall,
dark, and handsome, hair slicked back into a
ponytail with a half-smile just like my dad's. It made
me forget where I was and who I was. As far as I
knew I was this young boy in the drawing. Native
Americans are known for being brave and
adventurous and that's how I felt as I drew.

The seatbelt sign had come on with its little 'ding!'
so I put my sketchbook away and tucked the pencils
into the side pocket of my rucksack.

"Excuse me, miss. You need to put your luggage in
the overhead locker, please. We're coming in to
land," the flight attendant said to me with her fake
smile and face smeared in make-up. She reached her
hand out to take my bag away but I gripped it firmly
to my chest.

"Um…that's fine. I'll just put it away!" I snapped
back at her.

"Thank you, miss," she replied and walked off.

She was clearly just trying to do her job but my
sketchbook isn't something I want to be
sharing…Not yet anyway. I don't usually leave my
drawings unfinished because I like to draw in the
moment so that I don't mix other feelings with my

creativity, but I needed to prepare to build my new life, so the Native American boy was on pause for the moment.

Customs was tedious. How long does it take to identify who you are from the picture in your passport? Once I got past customs, I headed to the baggage collection. Hopefully, it wouldn't be a long wait. I only had two suitcases. Most of my clothes were for winter and rain so I didn't have many items for sunny California. Baggage collection was just as tiring as customs. Everyone just comes off their flight to stare at a rotating belt in the hope that their luggage comes out before the crowd comes along; hunched backs and saggy eyes. I just wanted my suitcases and then I'd be grabbing the first cab I saw.

After a depressing, ugly ten minutes, I got my luggage and headed out of the airport. There were people waiting at arrivals with signs. For some strange reason, I thought my name was going to be on one of those signs as if USC accepted me as a special student. But no, I was just daydreaming again.

Hailing a cab was pretty easy. I didn't need to whistle or yell, I just stuck my hand up as if I wanted to ask a question at high school and the cabbie parked right beside me. Sitting in the back of that cab, I wasn't trying to be ignorant but I really wasn't up for the 'small talk.' I was so anxious and excited to get to my dorm room and meet my roommate. I wasn't much of a people person. I'm quite shy meeting new people and a little socially awkward at times. I get that from my mother. My father was always the smiley, less serious person. That's what I loved about my pops; he always made me feel that I could be anyone I wanted to be; that it was OK to come out of my shell. From LAX to the USC campus it was about fifteen minutes so the nervousness kicked in very quickly. I just kept thinking about what my mom said before I left.

"They're going to love you."

I smiled thinking about it.

We pulled up to the residential halls. That sickly feeling was coming up again but this time it was mixed with excitement, so I tried to hold on to it. According to my schedule, I was in room 336 so I dragged my suitcases behind me and made my way up to my room. There were guys launching a football across the lawn and loud music was being played all over campus as I walked past. I tried to just walk past as friendly as I could and if I caught a smile I would give one in return. Everyone seemed so happy and excited. All I could hear was music followed by laughter, cheers, and the occasional grunts, seemingly from the football players.

"336…here we go," I said to myself, turning the handle on the door that already seemed to be open.

"Hey! You must be my roomy!" The exotic-looking girl, standing by her bed shouted over at me.

"Hi…" I replied smiling, feeling relieved and happy finally meeting my roommate. My hands started to slowly stop shaking as I eased myself forward to greet her.

"I'm Natia," she said, bypassing my handshake and placing her hands on my shoulders to give me a cultural kiss on either side of my cheek. It felt odd; it felt strange but it was new and friendly.

"I'm Elu…" I said back, smiling in awe as I looked at this beautiful girl, with her glowing olive skin and short, light-brown hair with golden blond highlights. Her eyes were big and she was so attractive that it seemed she couldn't possibly hurt anyone or say anything wrong.

"You're real pretty!" Natia said, slipping her hands off my shoulders.

I was in a slight confusion as to how this stunning girl could think *I* was pretty, so I kind of forgot what she'd said for a moment.

"Sorry? Um…Thank you. *You're* really beautiful," I said firmly as if she'd got it all wrong.

"So where have you traveled from, Natia?"

"A little island in the South Pacific Ocean called Samoa," she replied, grinning at me like she knew I was going to be shocked that she had traveled so far.

"Oh my God, that's a long journey…of course, that explains why you're so pretty," I said, going off subject.

Natia looked at me with such grace and humility.

"You're too kind. Thank you, Elu. What about yourself? You have a real nice name by the way." We both sat down on my bed cross-legged.

"Oh, it's… um… it's not like Samoa or anything, just a quiet town up north. Yeah, my dad named me after my grandmother. It means beautiful in his tribe's language."

"Tribe?" Natia said confused. Her face switched from an uplifting smile to a blank unable-to-understand face.

"Yeah…it's OK. My father has Native American ancestry," I said, reassuring her.

"Oh…I understand now. In Samoa, my tribe is called *Masina Nu'u*. It means 'people of the moon.'"

"So we're both tribeswomen!" I said to Natia, laughing. We both laughed and got to know one another as we unpacked and made ourselves at home.

'Knock! Knock! Knock!' Someone pounded on the door. Natia and I looked at each other and then I walked over to open the door. As the person at the door got the slightest of glimpses of our room from the other side, a voice shouted through, "Freshman dress-up-move-in party 11 pm!"

Flyers were shoved in my face with the scent of beer!

"Oh...Thank you!" I shouted down the hall as the guy ran shouting and chucking flyers at other students like a paperboy. I closed the door and leaned back on it. With a massive exhalation, I looked up at Natia with a smile.

"So...?" She was smiling back at me and I could tell Natia wasn't going to take no for an answer.

"But what would we go as?" I stupidly asked, like I didn't already know what we were going to be attending the party as.

12:30 am and an hour-and-a-half late, Natia told me how important it was to never turn up to parties on time for the cool kids and apparently we were the cool kids. Funnily enough, I didn't quite feel or look like a 'cool kid'. Here I was, in a Native American costume with a band tied around my hair and a feather poking out; red, blue, green and yellow face paint brightened up my pale skin and made my common brown eyes stand out. Natia was dressed in a grass skirt and a flower necklace and headband. She looked even more beautiful, but that was expected.

"Come on, El. This is going to be great. Let's get a drink and then you can show me how they dance up north!" she said, grabbing me by the hand and twirling me around.

Not that it bothered me, but no one ever called me 'El' except for my dad. Guess we were on nickname terms now. I didn't mention it to Natia but I'd never been to a party before and I definitely didn't know any fancy steps. I was homeschooled until high school when my grandparents forced my parents to let me breathe and go to school.

"Hey, 336!" I heard a shout over my shoulder. I turned round.

"I'm Adam. I live across the hall from you. Nice costume," he said, holding two cups. He was standing with bent knees so he could talk at my level without his voice being drowned out by the music.

"Hey, I'm El—"

"Who's this, El?" Natia interrupted, passing me a drink.

"It's um…Ad—" Again I was interrupted.

"Adam Lawrence and you're…"

"Natia," she said while lost gazing into Adam's eyes. "Natia Kelly…" she said and extended her hand for a welcoming handshake.

As if she was going to just put herself out there like that. I mean. Adam was tall, built, blond hair, blue eyes, pearl-white teeth and the Californian dream, but I wasn't going to be left by myself.

"Adam, it was very nice to meet you," I said very unconvincingly. "Nat, let's dance."

"Oh yeah…of course. See ya, Adam!" As I dragged her away she waved back at him.

We ran off onto the dance floor, laughing like two little girls in a park. The song playing was Dust by Eli Young Band.

"He was so cute!" Natia said as she stepped and slid to the music.

"Yeah, he was OK!" I shouted back.

"Oh come on, El! Live a little. I saw your cheeks blush when he came over!" She grinned back at me.

"They were not! It…it…it was the paint," I said, laughing back at Nat.

One day away from home and I felt like a new person already. Nat was amazing. She made me feel so lively and open to new things. I felt safe and comfortable with her. She saw the light in everything. She was just wonderful to be around and this was only one day with her.

The night was a great way to bump into loads of new people and being around Natia made it even easier to meet them because she made me feel like it was OK to be open and free; just how my dad would have wanted me to be. I knew somehow, that my dad wouldn't have approved of my fair share of tequila shots and my talking to friendly, attractive males, but I know he would be happy to see me smiling and being lively.

A couple of shots later…

"Aww, little Indian, let's get you to bed." Natia stroked my hair while my head rested on her shoulder.

"Yeah, that would be nice. Can we stop off and get some food? I'm a hungry, hungry hippo right now," I said, wiping the dribble off my chin.

"Of course! Pre-bedtime meal," she said as she helped me up to my feet.

We walked for what seemed like two hours to a little café called Ground Zero. It was on campus so it wasn't too far from our room, or it wouldn't be if you were sober. The place was quite full. Many of the students who had been out had come back there for food afterward.

"OK, what's this little Indian fancy?" Natia said brushing my hair off my face.

"Since the Mexicans kept me company with their tequila, I will have a burrito; chicken, no onions, and extra cheese, please," I babbled on in my drunkenness.

All of a sudden I felt this strange sensation running through my body and gravity left me from every angle apart from right in front of me. It was drawing me closer to a group of guys. I knew that if I didn't get out of the café, I was going to make a fool out of myself and be sick everywhere but the urge was irresistibly pulling me toward them.

I put my hands over my eyes and tried my hardest to block out the thought. It was working, so I slowly made my way outside.

"Here you go, my little Indian." Nat turned around and I was nowhere to be seen. She panicked slightly before seeing me outside. She rushed out.

"El, you OK? I've got your burrito," she said in her mellow, worried voice.

"No more Mexican for m—" As the group of guys walked out, the feeling came rushing back; the strange, lightheaded and pulling feeling that wasn't going too well with the alcohol in my body, because there and then, it shot up right from my throat and I was sick all over the corner of the café.

"Urgh!" Out it all came. How embarrassing.

"Aww, El, you're OK, I'm here." Natia was so comforting and sweet. I knew she would look after me. She pulled my hair back and took a napkin out of her purse for me to wipe my mouth.

"Can we go home now?" I said with my hand over my mouth and tears running through my face paint.

"Yes! Let's get you home."

Even after I had potentially ruined a good night out, Natia was still smiling and laughing. On our way home she was not embarrassed by me even though my face paint probably made me look like a clown at a kid's party. From that night on, I knew we would be best friends.

I felt a warm sensation on my face as the sun peeked through the blinds and shone his rays on me. I could smell the strong, sweet aroma of coffee. What a way to start the morning. Then out of nowhere, I felt as if death had come knocking on my skull himself, dripping a neat substance of hell into my brain, and delivering the most horrific hangover known to mankind.

"Nat, please, don't open those blinds and, please, whisper every single word as slowly as possible; the grim reaper himself is sitting right next to my head," I croaked out of my throat and turned my face into my pillow.

Nat pulled a chair close to the head of my bed and placed a cup of coffee on my dresser. The smell took my mind off the hangover for a bit but there was no chance I was ready to consume what was in that cup. Natia placed her fingers through my hair and combed, as if it was sand slipping through her hands. She giggled.

"El, don't worry. I'll look after you today" she whispered.

"Thanks, grass skirt" I chucked out there.

"Hey!" She stopped what she was doing.

I turned my face out of my pillow and squinted up at her.

"Just playing," I said swiftly. She smirked and placed her hand back on my head.

"Please, tell me we don't have anything important to do today. Grim's not going anywhere soon," I said holding onto my pillow. Natia placed one of those small triangular flags in front of me.

"I was thinking we would go watch the first pre-season game of the year," she said while waving the flag in my face.

"Ah…What time?"

"3 pm kick-off?"

"As long as you let me sleep till two-ish you have yourself a deal, Miss Kelly."

"Deal! GO TROJANS!" Natia shouted.

"Nat!" I shouted back.

"Sorry. Hangover, sorry," she apologetically said.

"Yay…Go Trojans," I mumbled.

I slept till around 2:15 pm and then Nat was sweet enough to pick some clothes out for me, including a USC hoody she'd gone and bought for both of us. I crawled out of bed and headed to the communal bathrooms with my clothes. The shower was so refreshing it brought back that memory of the rain back home.

"Elu, hurry up, we are going to be late!" Natia shouted over my cubicle.

"I thought it was good to be late?"

"Not for a football game. We will miss the good seats!"

After I got changed and Nat did my hair, we made our way down to the game. It was at The Coliseum, the home stadium for the USC Trojans. I'm not a massive football fan, not even a massive sports fan, but Nat enjoyed football. Her cousin Dwayne played for the University of Miami and did really well; she'd been watching the game ever since.

When we arrived there, the stadium was nothing like I'd ever seen before. This was all new to me. The stadium was huge. We made our way to our seats and the band was performing while being led by a guy dressed up as a Trojan soldier. They called the performance *The Conquest*. It was spectacular. The music sent shivers down my body and made the hairs stand up on my skin. If I had not been a Trojan football fan before, I was now sold, just on that performance alone; truly a 'wow' moment.

The Trojans were playing the UCLA Bruins, who were their main rivals so the game was intense. Once it began I could see why Natia was so excited about coming. A young man we'd met last night, by the name of Adam Lawrence, was a top prospect of freshman players and he would be playing today.

"This is something else, Nat. The atmosphere is incredible!"

"I know. Wait till we score and then it gets even better!"

You could see by Natia's enthusiasm and concentration on the game how much she loved the sport. As the game went on, there was cheering, chants and anthems by fans and the odd, "Get the hell out of here, Ref, with that bullshit call!"

It all came down to this. UCLA had offensive possession, fourth down and thirty yards to the touchline, with the game tied at 21–21 and twelve seconds left on the clock. Every single person in the stands stood up silently and still; not a word or a sound passed through anyone's mouth; not even a gasp of air was heard through those stands. Adam played defensive linebacker and he was known at high school for being one of the best in the country.

The ball snapped straight to the quarterback. He took three long strides back with all the offensive linemen blocking every single body in sight. The quarterback launched the ball with speed and power. It cut through the air fifteen yards down into Number 28's hands and as he turned around, there was Adam with his hands a couple of inches away from 28. Just when I thought Adam had stopped him, he handed Adam off to the side of his helmet, the firmest palm-to-head action you can imagine. Adam fell straight onto his ass and Number 28 ran straight to the touchline, raising the ball into the air.

No one could believe what had just happened. We all remained silent with heads being covered by hands and disbelief filling the stands. The final whistle blew and the UCLA Bruins claimed victory in rival territory.

"Nat...you OK?" I placed my arms around Natia's head and rested her head on my chest.

"We were so close." She trembled.

"I know. We'll get them next time!"

"Yeah..." She mumbled back.

The stands began to empty as the Bruins started cheering and celebrating on the field.

"Let's get you home, Grass Skirt."

As I took one last glance at the field, I saw Number 28 as he slipped his head out of his helmet and turned in my direction. That feeling from last night came back. I instantly started feeling really hollow inside and my center of gravity was pulling me toward him. My heart felt detached from my body and it felt as if it was being pulled by him in that direction. I gasped for air...

"Elu? What's the matter?" Natia raised her head off my shoulder.

"I...I...I...Ca..." I couldn't say anything; my voice just stopped.

"El, what's wrong? Are you OK?" Natia gripped both of my shoulders. She looked worried.

I couldn't say anything. I needed to know who this person was and what this feeling was. My soul felt an unconditional bond to this stranger and my heart felt as if it had been searching for this person forever.

He turned around and headed to the changing rooms with his team. 'Toa' was written above the 28 on his shirt.

"I...I..." The feeling started to go away but it had left an emptiness in my body like I'd never felt before. This was no silly schoolgirl crush. This was different. It wasn't normal. I didn't want to lie to Natia but I didn't want her to think I was a freak.

"Elu!" she snapped at me.

"I'm sorry, Nat...I guess the game got to me more than I thought it would," I lied unconvincingly, and if she knew it wasn't the truth, she didn't persist.

"Aww, I know. Let's do something tonight to keep it off our minds."

We headed back to our room; no victory celebrations tonight. What had seemed like a potentially great day had very quickly turned quite down and depressing. The campus was quiet and everyone seemed to just not want to talk, shout, or party. I guess it was more than just a game.

"Come on El, we are going out tonight!" Nat said in her joyful voice.

"Ah, Nat, I'm not really feeling up to it, to be honest. Think I'll just catch up on some sleep and finish off this sketch I was doing. I don't really fancy another episode of last night." I really didn't want to go out. I kept thinking about Number 28, Mr. Toa, and how I'd felt when I had seen him. It brought comfort to my heart thinking about him but when I stopped, a hole remained, needing to be filled.

"Nope, not going to happen! Plus, I have a surprise for you tonight!" she replied.

"Oh yeah, what's that? I hope it doesn't involve anything Mexican." We laughed. It didn't take a lot to convince me because I knew Natia would always look after me and lift me up, so maybe she would get this feeling out of me. So many questions and feelings I wanted to share with UCLA's Number 28.

We headed downtown to this little coffee shop that had an open mic night. Natia seemed to think it would be a nice way to spend the evening. It was very relaxed and calm inside. Everyone seemed to be listening to the poets or singers and enjoying their food and drink. I liked it; it seemed ideal for chilling out and potentially finishing off this drawing I had started back on my flight. We sat down and Natia looked up at me as if she was ready to interrogate me. I hope she hadn't figured out why I had been acting odd at the game.

"So?" She smirked.

"So?" I replied with wandering eyes.

"You going to show me your artwork or do I have to persuade you with a hot chocolate?" Relieved she hadn't asked about the game, I replied, "Hot chocolate? Sounds like a good start!"

"Marshmallows?"

"Pshh…Are you really asking me that?" I replied sarcastically.

As Natia went over to the till to order our drinks, I started to think about Number 28 again. The feeling soothed me and kept my body at ease. I felt hollow inside. I thought about his midnight black hair and his beautiful bronze skin; the way his dark mysterious eyes were kept directly away from my gaze.

"And he had a tat—" I blurted out.

"Who had a tat?" Natia replied, placing the drinks on the table.

"Huh? No one, I mean." She'd caught me off guard.

She looked at me.

"Do you have any tat's?" I asked, going off-topic.

"El!"

"Oh OK…I didn't want to say anything."

"Spill."

"Number 28 from UCLA last night..." My heart fluttered as I said 'Twenty-Eight'.

"Oh my God! Juliet, you can't be sleeping with the opposition!" Natia laughed.

"No...well, I...I don't know. I'm just being silly, aren't I?" I felt really awkward and didn't know where to put myself so I hid behind my mug of hot chocolate and started sipping. Maybe it would cover my shame.

"Oh, Ellie, I'm just kidding. If you like him, go for it! Just..."

"Just what?" I snapped.

"Just be careful. Those football players are known for being jerks, I wouldn't want to see you hurt." Natia placed her hand on top of mine as she said it, comforting me.

"I...Thanks, Nat. You're amazing!" I couldn't believe how cool and nice she was about it. There was literally nothing I could say to this girl that would make her not like me. She had a heart of gold at her worst.

"So, tat, ey? Typical bad ass?" She laughed it off.

"No, he had one of those traditional Polynesian tattoos, I think."

Natia stopped what she was doing and gave me her full attention.

"What do you mean? Did he look Polynesian? Did you see his name on the back of his jersey?" she asked, intrigued.

"Yeah...he...um...had one of those traditional pattern tattoos coming up his arm and on the back of his jersey it said 'Toa'."

"In my culture, if it's a real traditional tattoo, men get them to mark puberty and it also means they can speak for themselves and that they are ready to be warriors, which is ironic because 'Toa' means warrior in Samoan."

"Oh wow! So he must be quite respected among his family."

"Yeah...It's kind of a big deal," she said, grinning.

"Who would have thought?" I replied.

"Oh, Elu, don't worry. I'm sure once he notices you he'll be wanting your attention" she said while sipping from her mug. Natia looked happy for me. She kept reassuring me that it'd be fine and that things would work themselves out. I wanted to agree with her but I didn't see myself as a major 'hottie' or someone that could even get this guy's attention; plus, the fact that we were both at different colleges, and both were rival colleges, was just my luck, really.

I stuck my hand down into my rucksack to get my sketchbook out. If I was going to show Natia my work, this would be a good moment.

"Hope you like this." Natia stood up and walked toward the mic.

"Wait...what?" Oh God, she was walking toward the stage.

"Hi, everyone, my name's Natia Kelly. I've got a song I've been working on and I hope you all enjoy it."

Natia's mellow voice and charming character took center stage and the audience froze into complete silence. As she began to sing, I was amazed at what I was hearing. I couldn't believe this angelic voice that was coming out of her mouth that she'd hidden all this time. Her voice echoed through the souls of the audience and every single word and melody was clear and perfect. Her eyes were closed but it didn't take away from the performance because if you were looking at any part of her, it would be her lips and then you'd be lost in her lyrics and voice.

As Natia finished her song, people applauded and greeted her with friendly smiles and handshakes, as I sat there looking at my drawing. I felt uplifted and amazed by what I had just witnessed.

I could feel the presence of someone stood over my shoulder. I thought it was Natia but as I looked up it was him.

"Y—You. Wh—What?" There I was again, lost for words. This time it was different. Everything just seemed so surreal. Was I dreaming or was this actually real and actually happening?

As Natia walked over she glimpsed over at my picture and then smiled at the young man who stood over me.

"Hey, nice job, El. It looks just like him." She smiled and greeted this mysterious boy.

This was the boy in my drawing and as I sat there, in complete shock, he half smiled at me just like in the picture and just like my dad did.

"Oh, I'm so sorry. I'm Tate." He shook Natia's hand.

"Nice to meet you, Tate. I'm Natia and this is…" Natia waited for me to say something. "El?" Nat looked at me puzzled.

"I'm so sorry. I'm Elu…Do…Do I know you?" I said looking up at this boy.

"Uh…Not quite…Um, Natia, do you mind if I have a minute or two with Elu?" he asked politely.

"Yeah, of course! More hot chocolate?" She excused herself.

"Yeah…Um, yeah, cool, thanks," I replied.

Natia walked back over to the till. Tate sat down and placed both of his hands on the table. He sat there with this familiar smile on his face, his jet black hair tied up and stared straight into my eyes.

"I'm sorry. I'm just a bit confused by how you've come out of my sketch book."

He laughed. "I've been looking for you. I know this is going to come across very strange, but trust me."

How could I trust someone I'd just met? But I felt like I knew him and I did, because he was a part of my mind when I was escaping in my sketchbook.

"My name's Tate Chogan. I've traveled from a small town called Coldwater in Kansas. I'm from a tribe called the Comanche."

"OK…" I really wasn't sure where this was going but it was almost as if I had known Tate for quite some time.

"This is going to sound really creepy but you're the girl in my dreams," he said as he leaned over the table.

"What…what do you mean?" I laughed.

"Well, from about a year ago, I've consistently been having these strange dreams that revolve around you," he said as he toned his voice down.

"Seriously? Me? Why?" I started to become very concerned.

Natia walked back over with a tray of hot chocolates. She looked at me as if everything was fine, but it wasn't; this was all abnormal. Nothing seemed natural. I felt so out of place. I just needed to breathe. It was a lot to take in at once.

"Everything OK?" Natia said as she sat down.

"Yeah, um…I'm just going get some air." I stood up.

"Sure." Tate stood up in a very gentleman-like way; Natia smiled and gave me her reassuring nod.

How could this be possible? A person I'd drawn was a real person and that person was on a journey to find me because he'd had dreams about me. It seemed surreal. I wasn't sure how to feel about it, but my gut feeling was that Tate knew who I was and a part of me was telling myself I could trust him. Despite the fact I didn't know anything about this stranger.

Tate made his way through the doors, following me.

"Hey…" he said.

"Hey…" I replied.

"Elu, I know this is a lot to take in but…" He paused.

He'd gained my full attention.

"But…" He paused again. "The reality you believe in is a lie."

"What do you mean?" I just wanted him to tell me what he really meant. "Listen, you've come all the way from Kansas to tell me you've been having dreams about me, I don't have a clue who you are and—"

"But you do," he interrupted.

I paused.

"Elu..."

"No! Tate, I don't know who you are or what you want but you are seriously scaring me! Stop talking in riddles and come out with what you have to say!"

I started to become frustrated that he knew something he clearly wasn't telling me. I could see Natia through the window; she was keeping an eye on us. I nodded and smiled to let her know I was OK.

"Our ancestors lived in a time when things were very different. A man could take the form of an animal and could control fire with his hands; tribes would fight to protect their land and people. Our forefathers kept us hidden and protected from the reality of this so that we would respect and tame these gifts. As we age, however, our inner selves start to favor its natural way."

I could see by Tate's face that he was not lying, but how could this be? It's impossible for something like this to exist and be among us. It's just absurd.

"So you're saying that once I reach a certain age I can transform into a creature or start fires with my hands?"

"It's a bit more complicated than that. That's what I have come to talk to you about and this dream," he replied.

I stood there in complete shock, wondering what was going to happen to me. Then it struck me; I wonder if this feeling I had toward Number 28 had something to do with me changing but then again that would be completely ridiculous, this is the real world not some freak show.

"Sure... so what's going to happen to me?" I asked skeptically.

There it was again, that familiar half-smile.

"You're going to be fine, Elu. You're a strong person from a strong pack."

"Strong? Pack?" I didn't understand.

"Let me tell you about this dream I have been having; it will help."

We walked over to a bench and sat down. Tate gazed directly into my eyes.

"It starts with a pack of wolves and one wolf leaves the pack. As she begins to travel, she turns from a wolf into a coyote and begins her journey. As she comes across her travels, she meets a Red Indian in

the blazing sun and becomes infatuated with this
Red Indian. But this Red Indian represents the
undead and could potentially be bad for the coyote."

Lost in Tate's dream, I grabbed his hand and held it
firmly. It was absolutely insane of me to even give
this boy the time of day; he is a complete stranger
with a full of crap story, but then he pulled me into
him and held me and that overwhelming feeling of
familiarity returned; I didn't want to move. What on
earth am I doing and why am I giving in to this
stupid story, but the warmth and comfort of his body
kept me safe. I did not feel like I was putting myself
in danger weirdly enough; if what he was saying was
true, I wondered what was to become of my life.

"El, Adam's going to walk us back to our room,"
Natia said, standing in front of Tate and me.

I quickly raised myself off of Tate as if I was guilty
of doing something I shouldn't be.

"Um…You carry on, Nat. Tate and I have a lot to
catch up on."

"Sure?" she replied.

"Yeah." I smiled unconvincingly.

"OK, El. I've got my cell on me."

I smiled and Natia made her way back to the room
with Adam. Once she was in the distance, I cuddled
back up to Tate, I felt submissive and his bullshit

maybe not bullshit was just buried under my thoughts of this insane situation.

"There's so much I want to say and ask but I don't know where to start," I said as my head pressed against his chest and I looked up at him.

"I know," he replied.

"Like how do I understand this and how do I know you're not lying?" I asked, worried.

Tate raised me up from his body and as he slipped his hands into mine he said, "Elu, the truth is not written. The truth is in our hearts, the knowledge in our heads, and the beast is in our body. Tame the beast and all will become clear."

I looked deep into the eyes of this handsome Native American boy and felt at ease. Even though he'd told me something that from this point on would potentially change my life forever, I felt safe and I felt understood. Tate had the ability to keep my mind occupied. My escape became real but it was being shadowed by the lust of my unconditional feeling toward Number 28. My mind and heart craved these two men and I was lost with an empty body.

The next evening I wanted to meet Tate to talk more but he hadn't given me a number or any way to contact him. I decided to walk back down to the coffee shop where we'd met last night and there he was, leaning on the window of the shop and smiling in the distance.

As much as Tate kept me company, unraveled this massive secret, and made me feel like he was all I needed, I couldn't stop thinking about Number 28 from UCLA. The feeling was different. I had an urge and I needed to know what this feeling was. This was all so overwhelming; I knew that the feeling I felt for number 28 was not natural and quite possibly what Tate was saying had something to do with that, but I needed more proof.

"Hey, stalker," he said laughing.

"I see they've got jokes where you come from," I replied sarcastically.

He half smiled then placed his arm over my shoulder and around my neck cuddling me into his body. This is so weird for me, even now thinking to myself I've only known this guy for a matter of hours. We just casually began walking but I needed to ask him about this dream.

"Tate, you mentioned this Red Indian in your dream that could be bad for the coyote. What does it mean?" I asked.

"Oh…The Red Indians represent people of blood thirst and the coyote represents you." He turned away, trying to avoid the topic.

"Bloodthirst? What do you mean?" I replied.

"Cannibals, Elu. They're not people you want to be associating with," he snapped back at me.

"What are you hiding? Why can't you just be straight with me?" I snapped back at him.

"Just trust me."

"How *can* I trust you? I hardly know you, how do I know you are who you say you are? How do I *even* know you're telling the truth? I want to believe you… I… I… *think* I believe you, but… I can't trust you. I want to know what you really want!"

I became infuriated. My body became hot and I felt anger like never before. This was different. This wasn't normal. My temper was becoming uncontrollable, so I ran. It was weird enough that he looked exactly what I had sketched but his story was impossible to believe and why was he trying to hide parts of it from me if he really wanted me to take him seriously.

I got back to my room with tears running down my face and in a complete state. I slammed the door shut and slumped against it. I was in complete limbo. My mind and heart didn't belong to me anymore; an empty body that just felt lost and confused.

"Elu, what's happened? Are you OK?" Natia ran over to me and hugged me on the floor. She grabbed my face with her hands and rubbed my tears with her thumbs like my dad did. It helped calm me down.

"Nat… I'm so confused. I don't know what to say or where to begin." I sobbed trying to unload all my emotions.

"El, I can't help you if you don't tell me what's wrong. Take your time" Natia handed me some tissues.

"I don't know what to say…I'm being introduced to a world that I didn't want any part of or even know existed." I said while dabbing the tears off my face.

"What do you mean?" Natia replied.

"What would you say if I told you that myths and legends are not just tales and that those in them live among us?"

Natia paused and then after a couple of seconds of awkward silence spoke. "Do you mean like supernatural living?"

I looked at her face and from her expression. I could tell it wasn't the first time she'd heard this.

"Yeah…You know something?" I sat up.

"El…Some things are better left unsaid to protect people and in order to live a normal life." She turned away.

"Oh my God, Natia, you knew about this?" I leaned over.

"El…When you mentioned your family was from a tribe when we first met, I thought that you may know of this life but I didn't want to take my chances and ask." She stared out of the window looking at the dark sky.

She turned back toward me. "My family, my tribe, is from the Masina Nu'u, meaning people of the moon, like I said before. In ancient Polynesian mythology, my tribe believes that we are from a cultural hero called Tonga. They say he taught the birds how to sing. When my mother was pregnant with me, my father dreamt of birds singing by my mother's hospital bed. When my father asked a high chief about this dream, he said that I am a direct bloodline of Tonga and this is why they called me Natia, meaning treasure. That's why I sing the way I do. El, I didn't mean to keep this from you but we have to be careful who we talk to about these things."

It made perfect sense but what did this mean for me? I hadn't figured out who I was supposed to be.

"Wow…" I smiled at Natia. She knew this didn't change how I felt about her.

"But there's more. In my tribe, we are called the Moon People for a reason. It's because we have the ability to transform into wolves." She paused.

With my eyes wide and my mouth open in shock, I quickly remembered what Tate had told me about his dream.

"Nat, it's Tate…"

"What has he done?"

"No, that's how he came across me. He dreamt of a wolf turning into a coyote, which represented me. He said I would meet someone that would be trouble," I said with my eyes pacing back and forth, trying to remember everything he'd said.

Natia gasped.

"No, Nat, not you," I said at her worried face.

"No, El…if you have the ability to transform into a wolf, you need to be careful because it's hard to tame it to begin with. Has it already happened?"

"No…I haven't yet but what does the coyote mean?" I said curiously.

"I'm not quite sure but you need to talk to this guy. If what he is saying is true he'll know way more than I can tell you; he will be able to help you. He seems to know a lot."

"Nat, he's hiding certain things from me. I need to know the full truth."

Then it hit me.

"Nat, when Tate and I were talking, we got into an argument and it made me so furious, I could feel my body heating up and my heart felt like it was going to explode."

"You need to be careful; as someone who's never transformed before you can't lose your temper or else you will turn and it's hard to control it then."

As we both sat there sharing our emotions and thoughts about being gifted by our forefathers, I needed to share what I was feeling with Natia about Number 28. She might know something about this feeling.

"Nat, the other day when we were at the game, I felt this warm feeling and my body felt as if it was being pulled toward Number 28. It felt uncontrollable and my heart literally felt an unconditional bond toward him."

"El, if it is what I think it is, it's a bond you have with him. He could be your soul mate…that feeling is you yearning for him."

My heart felt comforted when Natia said this but my mind was thinking about Tate. I couldn't stop thinking about the bond *we* had.

"Are you sure?" I said.

"Yeah, of course, I've seen my brothers experience the same thing with their partners…which is a bit strange because it's usually only the males…" she said wonderingly.

"Yeah there's definitely something strange about all of this," I mumbled to myself sarcastically.

It was still a lot to take in; my transformation into a coyote, knowing there were others out there like me, an involuntary bond to my supposed soul mate, and my mind occupied with Tate. I still felt lost.

"El, souls were made in pairs. Go get him!"

Natia was so positive in every outcome. She saw the light in everything. For me, that was a gift in itself.

The very next day, I thought I'd take my sketchbook down to the park and finish off this picture with Tate in and see if any of it made any more sense. I found a nice little spot under a tree where I could take shade from the blazing sun.

I pulled out my sketchbook and began looking for a pencil in my bag but then I noticed a bird to the left of me; a fairly big black bird. I turned back to my bag to grab some food for the bird and when I turned back Tate was lying there on his back, staring into the branches of the tree shading us.

"Oh, my God, was that you?" I said in shock, grabbing my chest as if my heart was going to fall out.

He laughed, sat up and turned toward me. Then, with his thin long lips produced that trademark half-smile. I couldn't help but smile when he did.

"Yeah, that was me," he paused and smiled. "Listen, Elu, I'm sorry if I came across too harsh the other day. I just don't want to see you hurt; you're a very important person. You may not know it yet but you are" he said.

I scooted over, hugged him, and fell on top of him, making a small thud into his chest. We laughed and as I raised myself off him my hair dangled over his face. We had a brief pause as I looked into his dreamy eyes, then I noticed him raising his head toward mine and tilting his head as he started to close in on a kiss. I snapped back and punched him in the arm.
"That's for sneaking up on me!" That was awkward.

"Huh!" He sat up.

"I've missed you, Tate as weird as that sounds there is something about you that I really am convinced of but you need to let me in, you need to let me in to all of it," I said.

He smiled and I smiled back.

"You want to be careful with that sketchpad, El." He laughed.

"Oh... really? Why's that?" I laughed back.

We put our first argument behind us and started to bond. He told me about the many tribes of the native people and the many battles, feuds, and romances that our forefathers had come across.

"Tate," I said as I was twiddling with my pencil.

"Yeah, El?" he replied.

"I was wondering; if I come from a pack of wolves, why am I known as a coyote?" I started to shade the front of my sketchbook.

"Elu, there are many tribes of wolves that branched off from the Blackfoot Indians, who are the original wolf tribe. In the beginning of time, mankind lived freely and peacefully among the animal tribes. As the humans grew, however, they started to inherit ways in which they started to quarrel with the animal tribes over land and plantation. This formed into many fights, wars, and deaths on either side. The Red Indians decided that the world needed to be cleansed of these evil tenants so they plotted to rid all the creatures in the world and rule over the world as the master race. They set fire to the world and in the total carnage, very few tribes survived. They say the fire was so bad that the stars melted from the sky and crashed down into the earth. As this was happening, the gods disapproved of the Red Indians' doings, so they sent a massive flood to stop the fire. After the fire and flood, many lives were lost. All that was left was a destroyed world. Many animals and humans turned to stone, leaving the world in complete turmoil. As the remaining tribes fought for their lives, to survive and carry on their race, many died as a result of thirst, hunger, and uncleanliness.

Just when all seemed lost, The Great Coyote came from the land of mist and led mankind and the animal kingdom together, commanding the birds to scavenge for food and crops to survive. As the tribes began to gain a better position for themselves, The Great Coyote set laws for the land, for the tribes to follow and live peacefully.

The Red Indians didn't like what The Great Coyote had formed and wanted to kill him as they wanted to lead superior over the land. So they plotted to kill him as he was returning home from hunting. As he entered the woods of his territory, the alpha she-wolf he embraced as his partner was murdered. They say her pelt was entirely soaked red from where the Red Indians shed so much of her blood.

The Great Coyote ran in utter rage to the Crow tribe and told them what had happened and to take his she-wolf puppy to the wolf tribe where she would be safe and protected. One of the crows, on hearing this news, told The Great Coyote that he had seen the Red Indians climbing and running through the woods with blood all around their faces. The Great Coyote ran to the peak of the highest mountain in the land and cried and howled so loudly that the gods themselves felt the pain and disturbance tremble in their hearts. Upon doing this, The Great Coyote called the Red Indians into battle to avenge his partner. He fought a great battle against many of the Red Indians; decapitating heads, removing limbs, and inflicting total blood shed upon them but The Great Coyote was outnumbered as the battle went on. He was crushed around his ribs and choked to death by the Red Indians.
A great loss it was. Hours later, the wolf tribe had found the body of The Great Coyote and in sadness

and anger, they swore to forever be enemies of the Red Indians."

I could see Tate's face as he was telling me the story of The Great Coyote. He looked as if he'd lost his best friend. Distressed and saddened by the tale, I reached for his hand. Gripping it firmly, I could feel a tingling sensation. The best way I can describe it is if you could sense an emotion, that emotion would have been sadness.

"Tate...I...I'm sorry. I understand now why you got angry about me mentioning the Red Indians," I said.

Tate looked at me with his watery eyes and said, "I know, Elu, but it's our history. It's who we are. This is where you have a connection to all of this." He paused. "After this happened, the Red Indians declared war on anyone who wasn't a Red Indian. Many battles and wars happened and as a result, the Red Indians became stronger and bigger in numbers as they took over the land. The gods, in an attempt to help the animal tribes, gave them the power to transform into human bodies in order to become hidden among mankind—"

"Wait, what happened to The Great Coyote's daughter?" I interrupted.

"She became a fierce leader to the Blackfoot Indians and the alpha she-wolf of her pack. Her name was Migina. She fought off many Red Indians for her land and people. She was a cultural hero to many. The name Migina means the Returning Moon."

"So what relevance does this have for me?" I asked skeptically.

"What the Blackfoot Indians didn't understand was that when Migina was adopted by them, she hadn't been born a coyote; she was born a wolf."

I stared at Tate in confusion.

"But before she passed away she prophesized, 'One of you will become like my father when the time of trial and difficulties comes near. You will be forced to reconcile peace but it will come with a choice that will end in a great loss for the better of mankind.'"

In complete shock, my body froze, my heart raced, and my eyes leaked with sorrow and disbelief. I didn't want this. It wasn't fair. I had no control over my life and destiny. I knew that much of this big responsibility I had, was going to come with great sacrifice.

"No...No...Tate! No! It's not me! Why me?" I cried, pleading with him to tell me it wasn't true.

"Elu, this is who we are. You are the heir of The Great Coyote," he said.

"No, I don't want to be. I don't want your wars, your sacrifices, and your responsibilities." I screamed in sorrow, weeping into Tate's chest.

"I'm sorry," he mumbled as I felt his face frown on my forehead but then he suddenly pulled away and grabbed me firmly by the shoulders.

"Elu you are the one! Your tribe, your people and this world have been waiting for your coming… You are the one that is prophesized to end this darkness once and for all. YOU will put a STOP to this madness, and you will free and lead the people of tomorrow! I believe in you, as we all will; you are the heir to The Great Coyote!"

Learning to accept my ancestry, my heritage, and my future consumed my mind and my thoughts for the next couple days. I spent days daydreaming and wondering about what was to come; when would I turn? How do I control it? Who can I trust? These were just a few of the many questions that I kept asking myself.

"Miss Black, hello?" The teacher caught me daydreaming.

"Uh yeah…" I smiled trying to pretend like I hadn't been caught off guard.

"Miss Black, these paintings are wonderful but how about developing and processing them? You have been editing the same piece of work for the last couple of days."

I'd painted a coyote shielding a pack of wolves; her tail curled around the pack. It was all I could think about.

"Yeah…I'm sorry, I'm just a bit lost as to where to go next, in more ways than one," I said while rubbing my thumb over my index finger.

"OK, well, keep at it." She placed her hand on my shoulder and walked off to look at other students' work.

I just couldn't find any interest for my passion right now. I needed to know my purpose and where my future was heading. This was my main focus. I needed to get out of this class. I grabbed my paintbrushes and canvases and walked straight to the door. I knew my teacher would notice but that wasn't important right now.

I wasn't going to let this eat me up inside and determine my future. I was going to control it and overcome everything that could come my way, human or not human. I've never seen my dad scared or worried in my life. He is so brave and courageous and that is exactly what I was going to become.

I needed to let Natia know what was going on. I could trust Natia. Even though she'd hidden her abilities from me, I knew she had my best interests at heart.

As I walked outside toward my room, the sky seemed different. Previously, it had just been the sky in the background but now it was almost as if it was breathing. As the wind delicately brushed past my face, it felt as if my mom was placing her hand on my cheek to comfort me. The sky knew who I was. I felt a sense of its living. As strange as it sounds, I could accept that the sky was trying to communicate with me. With one spare hand free, I opened the other with my fingers spread to greet the wind and I felt a rush of air slip through my fingers. I had just communicated with the wind and it felt natural and beautiful.

"Nat!" I came rushing in.

She was lying on her bed, singing with headphones on. As I came in she pulled them down and sat up.

"Hey, El, what's up? Did you speak to Tate?" she asked.

"Yeah, I did. So it turns out that I'm the heir of The Great Coyote. Things are going to hap—"

"Wait...So what does that mean?" she interrupted.

"It means I have the ability to transform into a coyote but I haven't yet...But when I spoke to Tate he told me about this battle between mankind and the animal tribes against the Red Indians—"

"Red Indians?" Natia interrupted.

"Yeah, they're like cannibals and bloodthirsty people. That's what Tate told me." I sat on Natia's bed.

"Wait, El, this is all too familiar." She paused.

"What do you mean?" I replied.

"In Polynesian mythology, if I'm right about what I think you're referring to, the Red Indians are similar to the Malietoa Tribe, meaning 'great warriors.' These people were brave and fierce warriors—the protectors of the land—but when their first leader Malietoa Savea died, the next heir Malietoa Uilamatutu reigned superior over civilians. People that were not of their tribe were cast out and considered below them. Malietoa Uilamatutu was a cannibal and killed innocent people to feed on their blood and he turned an army into immortals that would feast on the innocent. The people of Upolu

Island lived in fear and terror as the Malietoa tribe killed freely. As the years went by, the Malietoa spread throughout Polynesia but when they came to Samoa, my tribe, the Masina Nu'u, fought back, as we had the gift to turn into beasts, like wolves, and we pushed the Malietoa tribe out. At the time, the Malietoa was led by a king called Malietoa 'Ula. He was a cruel leader who killed anything and anyone who wasn't part of the Malietoa. Even his own people lived in fear and no longer wanted to be a part of his kingdom.

In an attempt to escape Malietoa 'Ula's evil ways, many Malietoa called a truce with other tribes around Polynesia and left Upolu Island so long as they agreed to not kill any humans and only feed on the flesh of animals. The remaining Malietoa tribe and Malietoa 'Ula stayed host on Upolu Island and plotted to take over Polynesia, but upon hearing their plans, Hina the Moon Goddess cursed the Malietoa tribe and banished them to the underworld. As Malietoa 'Ula and his tribe were sentenced to the pits of darkness, he said, 'When my blood passes through generations, there will be a time when it will leave Upolu and you will not be able to stop it because of the innocence. Once it becomes of age, my blood will flow through its veins causing Ao-Toto and you will no longer have a hold over me, Hina! I will come after the Masina Nu'u and I will eat the flesh of your Alpha!'"

Natia looked as if she'd just witnessed a whole war in front of her. As she told me this story I could see the terror and horror in her eyes. I didn't feel scared but I felt like no matter what I did, people were going to get killed and I had no idea how to stop it or when this was going to start taking place.

"Nat, what's Ao-Toto?" I brushed Nat's hair back and wiped the tears from under her eyes.

"Cloud of Blood," she whispered.

"Huh?" I was confused.

"It's a sign of the coming of the Malietoa." She wept.

Natia's head fell straight into my chest and she began to cry again out of fear of what was to come. I felt uneasy but I needed to stay strong and not be broken by the fear of this evil. I squeezed my arms around Natia and placed my head on top of hers to make her feel that I'd never let her come to harm. It was hard seeing Natia like this as she was always so positive and happy, but the harsh reality was coming closer day by day and it was just a matter of time.

All this responsibility of living up to my native ancestors, the bond and emotions that kept my mind occupied by Tate, the lust for love my heart craved for Number 28, and the feeling of being unprepared for my future, plus juggling my college work was getting too much to handle. I needed to escape for a while.

I got up really early the next morning, still feeling that I needed to escape my life. Natia was fast asleep so I tiptoed around the room, grabbed my book bag, chucked on some clothes, and made my way down the quiet streets of California along with the creeping sunrays of dawn.

Not too far from campus, I came to a statue of a Trojan soldier with a shield and sword in hand and, of course, the Trojan helmet.

"This must be the Tommy Trojan that everyone always mentions," I said to myself.

The statue was really a piece of art. You could see all the muscles in the statue's body tense. He looked ferocious and brave. Under the statue there was a plaque that read, 'Faithful, Scholarly, Skillful, Courageous, and Ambitious.'

"Courageous and Ambitious," I read aloud to myself.

That's what I needed to be and it was what I was to become. I found a bench near, with Tommy Trojan in sight, and planted myself there taking my sketch book out to capture this icon. I opened my sketchbook up, flicking through the pages, and then I paused noticing the picture of the Native American boy that I had not finished. I stared at the picture for a while, remembering Tate. The boy in the picture was exactly how Tate was from head to toe; broad, tall, and athletic. Hair tied back, dreamy brown eyes accompanied by his beautiful half-smile. I paused. Was the sky talking to me again because it had started to remind me of Tate? Dawn was like Tate's smile; it was beautiful to see but it held back on showing you the full beauty. Like Tate's smile, the sun showed half of his beauty peeking through the sky but didn't produce the full body until time went on. But even dawn illuminated the darkness with only a fraction of the sun, reminding me of Tate. It was truly a beautiful feeling. It gave me hope. Tate's half-smile made me smile. Even though it was not his full smile, it still brought out happiness in me. I knew he hadn't told me everything I needed to know yet, but like the dawn, I was content with the fraction of beauty he gave.

As much as I felt troubled about the things that were happening and were to come, my negative emotions were always fought off. They were driven away by people, nature, or signs of positivity and hope. Maybe the gods were on my side. I finally had beautiful scenery and time to myself to finish off this drawing. So, as the beauty of the sun encouraged and inspired me, I began to draw the blazing sun to light the picture and give it hope. I was happy and satisfied with the outcome. It still wasn't finished but I didn't want to finish it. I felt a strong connection with this piece of work, more than with any other. It wasn't the right time to end the drawing, so as the sun ascended into the peak of the sky, I packed my sketchbook. I stood up and began to walk away, I smiled looking back at Tommy Trojan and seeing another side of the base that read, 'Here are provided seats of meditative joy, where shall rise again the destined reign of Troy.'

I embraced these gifts and attributes I was blessed with from my ancestry. As days began and ended I started to balance my student life with my new life. I accepted that what would become of me was written and my future would unfold when the time was near. I started to get back to my normal life during most of the day when I had lessons and course work. My passion didn't become a priority but it wasn't pushed aside either. It gave me hope, it gave me a break from a life of responsibilities and somehow made me understand and tame my new life.

"Miss Black, it's good to see you on top of your work. Your work ethic and quality of work are phenomenal. Please, do keep it up," my teacher praised me.

"Thank you." I smiled as I began to pack my things away.

Life was finally going in the right direction. Some things were still a bit unclear but I knew it would take time. It was about 2:30 pm and I'd told Tate and Natia to meet me at the Alumni Park at 3:00 pm, so I had thirty minutes to make my way down there and could possibly grab a bite to eat on the way.

"Heads up!" a voice shouted.

A football came blistering through the corridor and struck me straight on the forehead.

"Ouch! What the hell!" I said, squinting my eyes from the pain of the impact while rubbing my forehead.

"Are you OK? I'm so sorry." A hand reached out toward me.

As I looked up, I could see a perfect set of pearl-white teeth, and beautiful sky-blue eyes looked down at me. My face was turned to face his by big manly hands. My vision cleared up and it was Adam who stood in front of me.

"Hey, the Little Indian!" he greeted me.

"Huh? Oh! Hey," I greeted him back, shrugging his hand off my face.

"Sorry, India… We were just messing about and you managed to catch the ball with your head. You sure you're OK?" He laughed.

"What happened to 336? My name is Elu, and yes, I'm fine. I've got be somewhere, excuse me." I brushed past him as I walked away.

It wasn't the fact that he hit me with the football that annoyed me but more the fact that he was trying to be charming and flirtatious with me like he'd done with Natia the first night we'd met. I could see right through his act of kindness and notice the jerk he was.

"Anytime, Elu!" he shouted at me as I walked away.

As I walked past his group of friends I replied, "Yeah, sure…Aaron. I mean, Alan, or was it Aidan?" I said sarcastically.

His group of friends began laughing. I couldn't begin to imagine how embarrassed he must have felt but he shouldn't have tried to treat me like a piece of meat.

As I made my way to the Alumni Park to meet Tate and Natia, the sun was beaming on a very hot Californian day. It made me happy because it reminded me of Tate and when my mind was focused on him it kept me occupied so I wouldn't feel my urge for Number 28 from UCLA. Although I was getting used to the beautiful bright weather of California, I still missed the rainy days back home.

Walking into the park, I saw Natia sat down on the grass but I couldn't see Tate. As I walked toward Natia I heard a crow. I looked around me and then in the not-so-far distance, I saw that same big black crow again. He toddled along the branch and then glided behind the tree, and just like that, out walked Tate.

"Hey," Natia greeted me.

"Ladies," Tate said, walking toward us.

"Hey," I smiled.

"Nat, you remember Tate from the coffee shop and stuff?" I said.

"Yeah, Yeah...The guy El doesn't shut up about." She laughed.

"Nat!" I nudged her.

Tate laughed and then smiled at me. I couldn't help but be wooed by his graceful smile. We all sat down and began to talk.

"So, anyway, I've brought you both here today because I wanted you to meet each other and also talk about the supernatural," I said.

"Oh." Tate looked uncomfortable.

"Tate, it's OK. Natia is from a wolf tribe in Samoa," I reassured him.

"Really? That's interesting. What tribe are you from, Natia?"

"I'm from the tribe of the Masina Nu'u...The Moon People," she replied.

"And which of your gods do you follow?"

"Hina, the Moon Goddess," she replied.

As I sat there and watched the two talk, it looked pretty intense. I could see Tate was very cautious about Natia and Natia was just trying to help Tate understand to the best of her knowledge.

"Ah...OK! I understand now. You say Hina in Polynesia; we say Komorkis. Same Goddess, different names from different languages," Tate said as he came to a conclusion.

"I understand," Natia said as she smiled at Tate.

"So now we—" I said before being interrupted by Natia.

"But wait, who are you then?" she asked.

"I'm Tate Chogan. I'm from a small town called Coldwater in Kansas. I'm from a tribe called the Comanche, heir of the great warrior Tonto, and inheritor of the powers of the trustworthy people of The Crow," he said.

"Wow! That's one hell of an introduction," Natia said.

"Oh, don't forget smart-ass know-it-all by day and stalking blackbird by night," I laughed and added.

He winked at me and laughed. Natia laughed too. It was nice to have the most important people with me at the same time on the same page.

"Anyway, as I was trying to say, you both know my situation; some a bit more than others," I smirked at Tate. "But Natia has the ability to change from lady to wolf, and you, Tate, can change from man to crow. I'm meant to change from girl to coyote but I don't know how. I need you guys to help me. Tate, I think there's something more than being able to change into an animal that I can do. The other day I felt the presence of the sky. It was communicating with me."

As crazy as this would sound to anyone normal, I knew Tate and Natia would understand what I was saying or at least know that I was not losing my mind.

"Elu, that's nature." He smiled. "See, now that you're starting to realize and become who you really are, the elements of the world will reach out to you because they remember what The Great Coyote did for them and you're the next of kin," he added.

"Elu, the first time you change it's very hard to control yourself but don't worry, we will be there for you when it happens. It may happen when you least expect it but I have faith in you that you'll tame your inner self just fine." Natia reassured me.

"OK, great. I can tame it," I said to myself very unconvincingly.

"Natia, in the story, The Great Coyote led the wolf tribes to forever be enemies of the Red Indians. I know you said the Malietoa tribe tried to invade Samoa before the Masina Nu'u pushed them out but is this the same case for your tribe?" I asked.

"Yeah, kind of...It's like the Masina Nu'u and the Malietoa tribe have never liked each other," she replied.

"But what about the Malietoa that left Upolu Island to immigrate elsewhere? I mean surely there were Malietoa that came to Samoa?"

"The Malietoa live in Samoa too but they keep their distance from the Masina Nu'u. They have their own territories."

"Natia, sorry to interrupt you, but I think I know what you're trying to say, Elu. There are wolf tribes all over the world. Like I said before, you originate from the first tribe of wolves, The Blackfoot Indians. As time went on and the world aged, wolf tribes spread all over the world like the Masina Nu'u and just like the wolves spread so did the Red Indians, like the Malietoa tribe. Hope I'm not losing you here but these tribes are not specifically the only ones in the world. It's the creatures and animals that categorize themselves," Tate said.

"OK, so what on earth are the Red Indians and the Malietoa?" I replied.

"Well, I thought you'd figured this one out for yourself by now," he said.

Tate and Natia both looked at me like they were waiting for me to figure it out for myself and then I started to add it all up. The Red Indians killed The Great Coyotes' partner and there was a lot of bloodshed but one of the crows said that he had seen the Red Indians with blood all over their face. Tate had once said that they are bloodthirsty people and cannibals; the same as the Malietoa tribe. A cannibal king led them. He killed innocent people and feasted on their flesh to become immortal. The last thing Malietoa Ula' said was, 'I will eat the flesh of your Alpha.'

"Va...Vampires?" I stuttered.

"Yeah, El, vampires or as they are commonly known, immortals." Natia replied.

It was no more of a shock than people turning into wolves or birds, to be fair, but just another worry to add to the list. I had to stay brave and focused.

"Great, immortals," I said, as I stared into open space.

"You know what? I think that's enough for today. Don't worry, Elu, the more you know, the more you grow, the more it will all become clear to you," Tate said as he placed his hands on top of mine.

"Thanks, Tate." I smiled at his comforting words.

The next day, I woke up and ran down to the coffee shop for my and Natia's daily fix. It was my turn today. Once I'd come back with our coffee we both began to get ready for classes. It was fun sharing a room with Natia. I was an only child back home and I didn't have the company of a sibling so I shared these new experiences with Natia. We always helped comb each other's hair and pick out outfits for one another. During the day I hardly saw Natia as she was studying music at The Thornton School of Music and I was at the Roski School of Art & Design. They weren't too far apart from each other; about ten minutes. With the Alumni Park right in the middle of us, it was the perfect place to meet each other for lunch or after classes.

We both usually walked down toward our buildings together and split up on West 34th Street opposite the MacDonald Olympic Swim Stadium.

"Ellie, don't forget the big game tonight against the California Golden Bears," Natia said.

"Yeah, of course," I replied unenthusiastically.

"Come on! Get into the Trojan Spirit! I'll meet you at Alumni Park for…Let's say…four. The game starts at six," she replied very energetically.

"Cool. I'll bring the face paint." I laughed.

We made our separate ways to classes, clutching onto our books like typical students. Class wasn't anything special today. We were drawing a still human figure. The guy that stood before us naked was clearly confident with his body. I did pretty well although I couldn't seem to get his curly hair right.

"Ladies and Gents, that is all for today!" the teacher shouted to end the class.

As I was packing my things up, the guy that was modeling for us to render, came over with his robe tied around him.

"Hey, do you mind if I take a look at your work?" he said as he leaned over toward me.

"Um, yeah, sure…" It wasn't my personal work from my own imagination so I didn't mind too much.

"Hey! Not bad." He smiled.

"Yeah, I couldn't quite get the hair," I said while pointing at my drawing with my pencil.

"Nah, it's great. I'm Jason, by the way." He extended his hand out for a handshake.

"Oh, I'm so sorry, I'm El—" I was saying but was interrupted.

"Elu, yeah, I heard the other day when you and Adam…" He paused.

"Oh, of course…Yeah. Nice to meet you, Jason." I placed my fingers in his palm for a very lady-like handshake.

"Likewise…You should swing by the game tonight. It's a big one," he replied.

"Yeah, I was planning to."

"Cool. So I'll see you in the stands then?"

"Sure thing."

I wasn't trying to come off as blunt or rude but I really didn't want to seem like I was trying to be flirtatious with Jason. I'd got enough boy drama in my life already and I was not even in a relationship. As I left class and made my way down to the Alumni Park it was about 3:45 pm so I would be getting there just as Natia arrived.

Just my luck, I was still early, so I thought I'd check in on Tommy Trojan. As I started to walk toward the statue I could see a bird sitting on top of Tommy Trojans' shield. The bird started to caw and then I realized.

"Hold on…Is that you, Tate?" I asked the crow.

It began cawing again.

"Such a stalker." I laughed.

Luckily everyone was making their way to the game so there wasn't anyone around to notice I was talking to this crow. Then, as I was looking up at Tate in his crow form, suddenly two hands covered my eyes followed by

"Guess who?"

"Nat, I know it's you." I laughed. She had a very distinctive voice.

"What you doing talking to Tommy?" she replied.

"I wasn't. Tate's up on the shield." I pointed.

"Tate?"

Then the crow waddled from the shield onto Tommy Trojans' shoulder and cawed.

"Oh." She laughed.

"Hey, Tate! Fancy coming along to the game?" she added.

The crow flapped his wings twice and cawed.

"Take that as a no then." Natia laughed.

We headed to the game with our red-and-yellow face paint on with which we'd written Trojans. The crowd was large and there were a lot of noises and chants just like at the previous game.

"Hey, look, there's Adam!" Natia said.

"Yeah, I didn't tell you what happened, did I?" I replied.

"No, what happened?"

"He was being a jerk so I showed him up in front of his teammates."

She laughed.

"Yeah, I told you jocks are the worst kind!" She wrapped her arm around my neck and pulled me into her.

"I know." I laughed as I placed my arm around her waist and we jumped, shouted, and chanted as the game went on.

It was a one-sided game as the Trojans led 28-8. Natia and I were such great supporters. We chanted,

"Fight on for ol' SC

Our men fight on to victory.

Our alma mater dear,

Looks up to you

Fight on and win

For ol' SC

Fight on to victory

Fight on!"

It was one of the famous USC chants called *Fight On*. We even started a Mexican wave; it was so exhilarating. The atmosphere just magnified everything so much. Everyone was cheering and singing. It felt great.

"El, Stratford, Number 24 keeps looking up at you from the bench," Natia said.

"Who?" I replied.

"Number 24 keeps looking. Wait, you'll see."

I looked over and I could see the player sitting on the bench, and as he reached for his water bottle, he turned and looked over in our direction. It was Jason from class; he smiled and waved so I waved back.

"Oh look at you! Getting all this attention." Natia nudged me.

"It's not like that. He's just some guy that was in my

class today, plus I've already got a football player to worry about," I replied.

"Oh yeah, 28. What's going on with that, El?"

"I don't know…I really like Tate but it's like you said; if I'm supposed to embrace Number 28, then I can't get close to Tate and it's all just confusing, you know?" As I placed my head down

Natia raised my head up with her fingers on my chin.

"El, don't beat yourself up about it. If Tate occupies your mind and 28 holds your heart, go with your gut feeling."

She was right. Something my dad would have said. I missed him so much.

"I know, let's enjoy this game and worry about it later." I shrugged it off. I just wanted to enjoy being normal for a bit.

"Sure, Little Indian." We laughed.

As we left the game there were flyers being handed around about an after-party at Pi Kappa Phi fraternity house. Natia and I thought we would attend as everyone was in a great mood after the Trojan victory. We walked for about twenty minutes with the crowd to the after-party, arriving at a big white building with the writing ΠΚΦ on the building shadowed by a blue glow. It was just complete and utter chaos; alcohol was flowing freely, music was blaring, and people were dancing everywhere including the roof. Red and yellow colors filled the area with cheers, smiles, and singing.

Natia and I walked into the building and grabbed a drink from one of the tables. It was a typical 'red cup' party. We walked around and bumped into a few faces we recognized and then not long into the party the music stopped. I thought it was getting shut down by the police or something but then the DJ announced on the microphone, "Ladies and gents, let us salute our victorious Trojan warriors!"

In walked the USC football team followed by loud chants and screams. Everyone applauded them on their victory with first pumps, clapping, and hollering.

"Told you it would be fun," Natia shouted above my shoulder.

"Yeah, what an entrance." I carried on clapping.

They all came into the front room where the DJ was playing. All wore their red-and-yellow varsity jackets and each player was handed a drink. I could see Jason and Adam standing there together and I hoped neither of them would bother me tonight.

"El, I'm just going to answer this call. You're OK here, yeah?" Natia said as she held her cell phone with one hand and covered it with the other.

"Yeah...Yeah, sure. I'll be just here," I replied.

When Natia left, I went into another room to avoid any conversation with Adam or Jason. There were people playing beer pong, couples making out in each corner of the room, a bunch of guys taking turns drinking beer upside down from a keg, and I could have sworn, when I looked out the window, there were guys chucking toilet paper over the frat house from the front porch to the back garden. It was out of control. I needed to use the restroom so I headed up to the first floor, but of course, halfway up the stairs there was a massive queue. As I headed back down I heard one of the guys say, "You'd be better off finding a bush."

'How classy,' I thought to myself. I walked back down into the front room, where the DJ was playing, to wait for Natia. Then Adam caught me there and approached me.

"Little Indian, you're looking pretty hot tonight. Didn't think this would be your kind of thing." He came straight up into my face placing both hands on my waist with the stench of alcohol occupying his breath.

"It's Elu, jerk! Let go of me!" I pushed him on the chest as I turned my face away from his presence.

He gripped me in closer toward him; our waists were practically knitted together, and then he leaned over into my face.

"You think you're funny, don't you? Showing me up in front of my teammates!"

"LET GO OF ME! YOU'RE DRUNK!" I shouted as I tried to wiggle out of his clutches.

"No! Let's see how funny you are now!" With his hands gripping me tight he tried to push himself on me, persisting for a kiss.

"NO!" I shouted as I clenched my first as hard as I could and with all my power and my body tense to the maximum of my ability, I swung a punch straight at his eye.

Adam instantly let go of me and placed his hands on his eye, holding his face from the pain of the punch. The whole room froze and stared at me as if I'd committed treason against their king. I rushed to the front door but it was being blocked by drunken guys doing pull-ups on the door frame and shouting at each other. With a fast pace, I went into the room where they were playing beer pong. There was a window in there. If there wasn't a back door nearby, I would just climb out of the window. As I walked toward the window, I saw the back door just a few paces away. I walked toward it but a hand extended in front of me, grabbed the door handle, and slammed it shut right in front of my face. I turned around and Adam stood over me furious; veins pulsing on his forehead, and blood dripping from the side of his eye.

"YOU AIN'T GOING NOWHERE!" he shouted at me.

My body began to shake and I started to panic but I wasn't scared of this jerk. I took a couple of steps back and then he placed both of his hands on my shoulders really firmly. I wasn't scared to hit him again.

"TRYING TO SHOW ME UP AGAIN, AREN'T YOU!" he shouted.

As I clenched my fist again ready to throw another punch at Adam's pretty face, a hand gripped his arm and flung his body away from me. It was Tate.

Tate and Adam stood opposite each other. It was so intense. Tate stood there broad, tall, and ready to attack anyone who laid their hands on me. The room fell into utter silence. Everyone was staring at Tate and Adam. Natia came running into the room looking worried. I placed my hand on Tate's shoulder and I could feel his body trembling with rage

"Tate, leave it. Let's go home," I said.

Tate turned around to look at me and then Adam charged toward him.

"TATE! WATCH OUT!" Natia shouted.

Before Adam could make contact, Tate moved his body out of the way and propelled Adam into the window, making him crash through into the backyard. Screams and shouts filled the house and then two football players approached Tate. As one swung for a punch, Tate ducked and then followed up with an elbow to the bottom of the player's chin and knocked him unconscious. The other jock decided to swing a bottle at Tate, who slipped his head out of the way of the bottle, and then with a sudden movement grabbed the jock's arm and forced his strike into the wall, causing the bottle to smash and pierce broken shards into the jock's hand. In excruciating pain, and with a lot of blood gushing from the hand, he fell to the floor, screaming in agony.

I screamed as a shard caught the side of my face and left a small wound. Natia ran over and shielded me into her safety. I could feel the shaking of her body. We needed to get out of here. Natia was going to turn into her other form.

"STOP!" Jason shouted.

Adam came rushing in from the backdoor to be held back by Jason.

"Tate, we need to leave now!" I shouted.

Tate stood there, still squaring off to the football team with his back toward me; he looked like a mountain that couldn't be moved.

"TATE! NOW!" I shouted.

He turned around. His face was enraged; his jaw was clenched and his eyes were pitch black in an inhuman-like form. He stepped away from the scene and led us away from the fight and the frat house. As we got outside, Natia was still trying to hold off from transforming but she was only becoming more uncontrollable and her body increasingly shook.

"Nat, it's OK. We're going to get you somewhere

out of sight." I gripped her hands tight. This situation was beginning to make my hands sweat.

"Tate, we need to leave now!" I desperately shouted.

"The beach! The beach, Santa Monica…Go there!" Natia gasped her words.

"That's forty minutes away. We won't make it in time!" Tate shouted.

There was no time to be arguing so I hailed a cab down and we all got in.

"Santa Monica pier, fast!" Natia shouted at the cabbie.

"I'll go as fast as I can, ma'am," the taxi driver replied.

"NO! STEP ON IT NOW!" she screamed. An animalistic voice screeched through her normal voice.

The driver really did put his foot down, the poor guy. We got there in just over twenty minutes. Natia was in pain. She was holding it back so much that her eyes changed while we were in the cab. They went from brown to a bright yellow with hints of gray. I kept reassuring her that we'd be there soon. She moaned in agony, making the taxi driver really go as fast as he could.

"Nat, we're almost there now. Just hold on, OK?" Tate said, leaning over from the passenger seat.

"What do you think I've been doing for the past thirty minutes!" she shouted back. Her voice was beginning to change in a very deep and non-human-like way.

"What the hell is wrong with you kids?" the taxi driver shouted, trying to keep his concentration on the road.

"Just drive!" I shouted back.

As soon as we pulled up, Nat flung the car door open and ran down the stairs of the pier. I ran after her as she ran across the sand toward the shore. She started to transform; fur burst through her skin on every part of her body. Her figure broke out of her human exterior; her feet and hands sprouted into paws and her spinal cord shot through her body, extending her spine into an astonishing golden bronze tail. She then sprinted off onto the beach.

She was off into the night and out of sight. I headed back up to the top of the pier. As I did, Tate came running down the stairs.

"Is she OK? Where is she?" he said in a worried tone.

"She's OK, Tate. She sprinted off down the beach. I'm sure she'll be just fine," I replied.

I knew Natia would be fine. She just needed her own space and time. It was a lot to see and take in but it was something I was becoming a part of so I had to get used to this impossible fact. Tate and I walked back to the top of the pier where we looked over the barriers into the ocean.

"Are you OK, Elu?" Tate said as he placed his arm around me.

"Yeah…I'm fine," I replied, staring into the ocean.

"I know this was your first time seeing the transformation. You sure you're OK?" he replied.

"Yeah, Tate, I'm fine. Just a bit shocked. Like we talked about it all the time but seeing it right in front of your eyes is a different story."

"Yeah…You get used to it." He turned me around so I was facing him and as I looked up at his face he half smiled and kissed my forehead, wrapping his arms around me into a tight hug.

The next morning I was woken up by the smell of wet dog. I turned around and Natia was lying on her bed half-naked and looking as if she'd been living in a bush. I shifted my legs out of the gap between my bed sheets and placed my feet on the floor. As I stood, trying to be as quiet as possible, I tiptoed toward Natia and lifted her covers over her to keep her warm. She smiled and opened her eyes.

"Thanks, El," she whispered.

I smiled. "It's fine. Are you OK?" I whispered back.

She sat up and kept the bed sheets covering her body.

"Yeah, I'm alright. Sorry about last night."

"Don't be. You've got nothing to be sorry about," I replied.

"Yes, I do. I haven't turned into a wolf for a long time. That's why I couldn't control it more. Sometimes it just takes over you and no matter how much you hold it back, it just keeps fighting you until you change."

I kept silent for a moment.

"I'm sorry, Elu. I don't mean to make you scared. It's just something you need to know. From time to time you need to change; otherwise, it can just spring up on you."

"No, Nat, it's fine. I understand. Where did you go last night?" I replied.

"I kept running until I got to Santa Ynez Canyon Park; then once I was out of sight, I just wandered around the mountains and I came across this waterfall, hence the smell." She laughed.

I smiled at her telling me this and then I sat down on her bed and cuddled her, sharing her wet-dog smell.

"It was so reviving being able to be in my wolf form. I haven't changed since I've been here and the Canyon Park is perfect to get away and change because not many people were in sight, plus it was nice to roam around. Once you've transformed and you get used to it, I'll take you up there."

"Yeah, I'd like that. So listen, I'm going to run down to the coffee shop. I could do with one and I know for a fact you could too." I laughed.

"Good shout, El. I'll jump in the shower now" she replied.

I threw my USC hoody on and some flip-flops and ran down to the coffee shop. I knew Natia could do with the coffee after a long night. On my way and on the way back, I don't know why, but I was kind of expecting Tate to be flying around or to mysteriously bump into him but I didn't.

As I opened the door to our room I could hear Natia singing. It made me happy. She had such an amazing voice. It truly was a gift.

"Hey, Ellie. Thanks." She cupped her hands around the hot coffee.

"No problem." I sat on my bed and started to sip my coffee.

"So, El, I've got a bit of an issue I was hoping you would be able to help me with, if you can?" she said.

"Oh…yeah, sure. What's up?" I replied.

"So, last night that phone call I had, it was my auntie. Thanksgiving's coming up and, well, I can't go home for it because home's a bit too far, so I was wondering if I could spend it with you?"

I hadn't even thought about Thanksgiving yet and I hadn't spoken to my parents in so long that they must be so worried about me. I didn't want to go all the way back home either because we broke up from college on the Tuesday and that Sunday the Trojans would take on UCLA; if I had any chance of confronting Number 28 then it would be that Sunday.

"I wasn't planning on going back home either, Nat, so we'll do something here," I replied.

"Are you sure?"

"Yeah, of course. I'll somehow get hold of Tate and we'll have our first Thanksgiving together."

Natia smiled, came across the room and hugged me.

"Thank you, Elu, you're so thoughtful," she said.

"It's fine. I'm not cooking though!" I laughed.

I needed to ring my parents to see if they'd be OK with me missing Thanksgiving and just generally speak to them, as I hadn't spoken to them in so long.

Later that day, Nat was practicing a song she was working on for class so I gave her some space and headed back down to Santa Monica Pier. I thought I'd explore around the beach and hopefully bump into Tate. He didn't carry a cell phone and God only knew where he lived, so I was always waiting for him to find me.

As I walked along the pier, I thought it would be a perfect time to ring home, so I took my cellphone out of my bag and dialed home.

"Hello?"

It was my Dad. "Dad, it's Elu," I replied.

"El, are you OK? Why haven't you called your mother? She has been worried."

"Sorry, Dad, I didn't mean to. I've just been so busy."

"That's OK, as long as you're fine. How's college? You staying away from them boys?" He laughed.

I missed my parents so much, especially my dad. It made me emotional hearing my dad laugh. I paused to catch my breath and as I did so, a tear rolled down from my eyes, making its way down my face.

"Elu…Are you OK? What's the matter?" My dad knew I was upset.

"Nothing, Dad…"

"Elu Black, do not lie to me."

I wanted to tell my dad what was going on so badly. I knew if I could trust anyone it was him, but as much as I wanted to tell him, I couldn't because I knew that doing so could put his life and my family's life in danger. The chance was that if I told my parents about this supernatural life they would most likely put me in a mental hospital, or worse, they would come to me in L.A. meaning that if any of these bloodsuckers know where I am right now, my family would be in danger being around me. I just couldn't risk that.

"I just miss you, Dad…Classes are fine. Everything is really nice here. I've met loads of new friends." I didn't lie but it wasn't what I wanted to say.

"That's good, baby. Your mother and I miss you as well. Listen, your mom wants a quick word with you. I'll speak to you soon, baby. Look after yourself. I love you, and call more often."

"I love you too Dad and I will."

"That's my girl. OK, here's your mom."

The phone made a shuffling noise from where my dad passed the phone to my mom.

"Elu?" she said.

"Hey, Mom," I replied.

"Elu, are you OK? How's everything going there?"

"Everything's fine, Mom. I miss you guys."

"I know, baby. We miss you too. Don't worry; we'll see you for Thanksgiving."

Now I had to break it to them. "Oh, Mom, I won't be coming home for Thanksgiving."

"What? Why?"

"I've got a lot of work to do and I kind of promised my roommate that I would do Thanksgiving with her because she's a long way from home too."

"Oh, Elu, that was nice of you. Grandpa and Grandma miss you loads. Everyone's always asking about you."

"I miss them too, Mom. Tell them all I'm thinking about them too."

"I will do, angel. Well, make sure you call us on Thanksgiving Day, OK?"

"I will do, Mom. I love you. Bye."

"Love you too, Elu. Bye, baby."

As I cut off the phone and was staring at the screen of my cell phone, a hand brushed the side of my face and wiped the tears away.

"You OK, El?"

I knew that voice. I turned around and instantly hugged him. It was Tate. I stopped crying, I just needed a moment of comfort.

"Miss home, ay?" Tate said into the top of my head as I snuggled my face into his chest.

He tried to gently pull me off but I gripped tighter onto him. I didn't want to let go just yet.

"Don't want to come out just yet?" he joked.

I kept hold of Tate with my face smothered by his chest, hiding my sorrow, and he began to start walking with me still attached to him. I had to move my feet as well otherwise, he was going to fall on top of me.

"Well, you stay there. I'm hungry. Food?" He stopped walking.

I raised my head out of his chest with my arms still wrapped around him and looked up at his handsome face.

"I'm hungry too." I laughed.

He laughed.

"Tate, don't ever leave me. I need you."

He smiled and slowly leaned down, kissing me on my forehead with his soft lips. "I'm always with you, Elu."

I smiled because I knew he was always there, even

when I couldn't see him. It wasn't creepy or weird; he was my protector; my guardian angel.

"We need to get you a cell phone." I laughed.

"Um…I'll pass." He smiled.

We walked down to the pier until we found somewhere to eat.

"Hot dog stick?" he said.

"Yeah, sure." I smiled back at him.

"Weird, I've never actually seen you eat before," I said.

"You want to watch me eat?" He replied.

I laughed. "No, I mean like—" I was interrupted.

"Like do I eat normal food?" He laughed.

I squinted my eyes in annoyance and he laughed once again.

"So, Tate, I need to ask you something?"

"Yeah, sure, go ahead." He stopped eating and gave me his full attention.

"Natia and I were wondering if you wanted to spend Thanksgiving with us."

"Oh…um…you do realize Thanksgiving is this Friday, right?" he replied.

"Yeah...I know it's kind of last minute and, well, Natia can't exactly get a plane back to Samoa for Thanksgiving and I didn't want to go back home and leave her by herself. Please?"

"Yeah, I mean, I'll have to let my friend know I'll be bringing two extra guests but, yeah, should be fine. In fact, it will be great." He smiled.

"Oh really? Where are we going?"

"To celebrate Thanksgiving the proper way. You'll see."

As the sun came down and the stars started to come out, I was leaning over the barriers once again and staring into the stunning sunset with this attractive young man by my side. His half-smile mirrored the sunset's image and we just gazed into the sky, enjoying each other's presence.

Early that Wednesday morning, the holidays were upon us. The campus was decorated with a load of Thanksgiving-related images and decorations; turkeys, Native Americans, pilgrims and of course, the national flag. Natia and I sat outside waiting for Tate. He'd said to wait outside the campus and he would pick us up, but as far as I knew he didn't drive.

"El, what car does Tate drive?" Natia said.

"I don't know. I didn't even know he drove," I replied.

"Oh, this should be fun. Do you even know where

he's taking us?"

"Um…"

"Elu! Come on, you can't be serious?" Nat looked pissed.

"Don't worry, Nat, it will be cool. He said we were visiting his friend and that it would be great." I couldn't see Tate anywhere in sight.

"Great…" Natia replied.

An off-yellow, rusty Chevrolet truck pulled up right beside us and the sound of metal rubbing against more metal greeted us.

"Ladies, you ready?" Tate shouted over the sound of the truck.

Natia looked at me, I shrugged my shoulders, and then she instantly burst out laughing. She wasn't one to cry about things so when things didn't look too great she just laughed.

"Chuck your things in the back and hop in!" Tate shouted.

As we both jumped into the front of the truck, Tate had a massive smile on his face.

"Hey," I said.

"Hey, Tate," Natia said.

"You girls ready? We got a bit of a drive but it will

be worth it."

"How long is a bit, Tate?" Natia replied.

"Um…give or take, eight, maybe nine, hours." He pushed his fingers through his hair, then he rubbed his neck and looked away.

"Eight hours! Are you serious?" Natia shouted.

"Yeah, but it will go quickly. Don't worry. It's 7 am now; we should get there for 3 pm." He pushed the emergency brake down and began to drive.

Natia tapped her shades down from her head and stuck her feet outside the car window.

"Tate, where did you get this car from?" I said.

"Well, I had to make my way down there early yesterday morning and then I drove back in the evening," he replied.

"Wait, so you haven't slept? And how did you get there?"

"Crows are known to sleep with their flock. My flock is back home in Kansas. I flew there, of course."

"Oh, of course, you flew there. Well, we are your new flock now so how about you get some sleep and I'll take over for an hour or so."

"El, it's fine. I'm OK—"

"Nope, pull over. You're getting some rest!" I demanded.

We pulled over at the next gas station. Natia was already fast asleep as Tate and I traded places. Tate smiled and whispered as he fell asleep.

"Red Bear will like you, Apisi."

Apisi. I hadn't heard that name before. I drove for about two hours to just by Bakersfield and then Tate took the wheel again until we got to Shasta near Pit River, a village close by. We pulled up and a very tall, built man came toward the truck to greet us. He had very dark, reddish-brown hair.

"Greetings, friends," the reddish-brown-haired man said.

We all hopped out of the car and presented ourselves to this friendly man.

"Hi, I'm Natia. Pleased to meet you." Natia shook his hand.

"I'm Elu. Thank you for sharing this holiday with us," I said.

The man with the reddish-brown hair smiled and looked at Tate. Tate smiled back.

"You're more than welcome. Thanksgiving is every day of the year for us. We like to be helpful and giving to everyone. My name is Red Bear. I'm the leader of the Achomawi people here in Shasta," he said.

"Tate has told me all about you two and I'm pleased and honored to have you both here with me, especially you, Apisi," he added.

"Apisi? What does that mean?" I replied.

"Apisi is the name the Blackfoot Indians called The Great Coyote," Tate said.

"Oh...I'm honored, Red Bear. Thank you," I said.

Red Bear walked us around his village. There were big, cone-shaped houses that were made from bark, grass, and tule. The women were sitting outside the houses doing chores such as repairing clothes and cooking. There were small children running around with branches play-fighting and little girls singing while watching their mothers cook.

"Elu, Natia, would you like to join the ladies in preparing the feast for tonight? It's a tradition that the men go out to hunt and the women prepare the food," Red Bear said.

"Yeah, that's OK with me," I said.

"Me too," Natia added.

"Great." Red Bear smiled and then this beautiful light-brown haired woman approached him. She had a black line tattooed under each eye and three black lines tattooed under her mouth.

"Ladies, this is my wife Aiyana. She will show you around," he added.

"Apisi and Natia, please, follow me this way," Aiyana said.

"Oh…Elu is fine, Aiyana, really," I replied.

"It's a great honor to be called Apisi, Elu. You should accept this," she replied.

Natia looked at me and smiled. She placed her hand on my shoulder to say it was OK. We made our way toward the other women cooking around the fire. All the women wore clothes quite similar to the men's. Deerskin dressed them in gowns and skirts with embroidered patterns and colors that brightened up their apparel.

"Aiyana, you have a really nice name. What does it mean?" Natia said.

"It means Eternal Blossom. Thank you, Natia," she replied.

"That's fitting for such a beautiful woman as you," Natia said.

We began chopping vegetables and Aiyana and the other tribeswomen were skinning the meat and attending to the fire. There were three young girls with what looked like leaves stuffed up their noses. They were dancing and singing, making instrumental music with a rattle. It fascinated me so I asked about it.

"Aiyana, these three girls; why are they singing and dancing, and what is that in their noses?"

Aiyana smiled and then said, "Apisi, these girls are becoming women. This is the ritual they perform. The herbs in their noses are blocking the smell of the meat out because they are fasting," she replied.

"Fasting? What do you mean?" Natia said.

"They cannot eat until the ceremony starts tonight. When they perform a ritual dance and sing around the fire they will become women and they can eat and join the rest of the tribe."

"Oh, I understand now. Do all the girls of the tribe have to perform this to become women?" I said.

"Yes, Apisi, it's a sign of maturity and becoming their own person." Aiyana smiled and moved the meat into a pot to be cooked.

"Natia, Tate tells me you are of the wolf people? Is this true?" Aiyana said.

"Yes, in my home country we are called the Masina Nu'u, meaning the Moon People," she replied.

"Would you be willing to participate in a game tonight after the ceremony?" Aiyana asked.

"Sure, what is it?" Natia replied.

"It's more for the children but they will go and hide and the wolf and the bears seek them out, almost like we are hunting them, and then when the last child is left he or she is named 'Molimo,' meaning 'Bear walking into shade.' It's a great title for the children to earn."

"Yes, of course, it would be my honor to be part of your traditions." Natia smiled at Aiyana's request.

I couldn't help thinking that there was so much to this other life; new people, new traditions, and new abilities that were yet to be discovered.

"Don't worry, Apisi. I know you haven't taken your natural form yet but we will still need your help in the children's game," Aiyana said.

"Oh…really, how so?" I replied.

"When the last child is to be found, all the women go out to look for the child to greet him or her with the winning title."

"Yeah, sure, I'd be up for that."

Natia, Aiyana, and I carried on cooking with the rest of the women; chopping vegetables, skinning meat, and keeping the fire alive. The men eventually came back with a few more rabbits, fish, and deer just before sunset. Red Bear and the Achomawi tribe were very big built men. They must have inherited that through their tribe plus their natural form of being bears.

Tate walked over to me.

"Catch anything for the feast?" I said.

"Ah…as a crow, I watched over the woods and gave the men directions to where the prey was heading," he replied.

"So you didn't catch anything?"

"Uh…well, technically—"

I began laughing and as I interrupted Tate he laughed with me.

"Come here, I want to show you something." I grabbed Tate's hand and led him past the tall trees to an open view of the sky where the sun had begun to fall into the river.

"It's beautiful, isn't it?" I said.

"Yeah…" Tate gripped my hand a little tighter.

He didn't know how the sunset reminded me of him and how I was attracted to him, but I didn't want to show him because I was scared of losing him to someone else; someone that no matter how much I tried to block out, the feeling of him consumed my heart…Number 28.

Tate linked his fingers into my other hand and turned to face me; our eyes locked into each other. The warmth of his breath stroked my lips as he slowly moved his face closer to mine. His fingers released my hand and hovered and then cradled my face. As I could feel his heart pounding through his fingertips and onto my face, a small gap between his lips and mine was left to conquer.

"Apisi!" one of the tribe girls called.

We both stepped away from each other upon hearing the tribal girl.

"Yeah?" I replied.

"You must come quickly. The ceremony will start soon. You need to change your clothes," the tribal girl said.

"Oh…OK…Yeah, sure, I'll be right there."

Tate scratched his head, looking in the other direction out of embarrassment.

"I'm…I'm going to let you get ready…" he said.

"Yeah…I probably should…I'll see you," I stuttered.

"Yeah, yeah, I'll see you in a little while," Tate replied.

After that awkward moment with Tate, I headed to Aiyana's house where Natia and I got ready and were dressed by the tribeswomen. They dressed us in beautiful robes with deerskin and embroidered colorful accessories that acted as jewelry.

"Apisi…" Aiyana raised her hand to her mouth and gazed at me.

"What? What is it?" I replied.

Natia walked into the room with her traditional Achomawi attire.

"Wow…Elu, you look great," Natia said.

"Apisi, the clouds will cry a flood of joy and the sun

will melt out of lust upon looking at you," Aiyana said.

"Wow, thank you…" No one ever made a big deal out of the way I looked and these words truly touched me.

We headed outside to the fire where the men were already sitting and the three girls from earlier were kneeling on the floor, waiting to perform. All the women sat opposite the men. When the ritual began, the three girls began singing and dancing around the fire. The tribeswomen joined in and sang with the girls. It was spectacular; a truly amazing experience. When the girls stopped dancing and singing, they sat in front of the tribeswomen and three men approached them with a bowl of fruits and nuts and they ate. Once they all took a bit of food, the men cheered and chanted and so did the women.

Red Bear stood up and announced, "Brothers and sisters, today we celebrate three more girls becoming women! Welcome our guests into our homes and let us eat together!"

All the women rushed over with a bowl of food for their rightful partners and the men and women sat and ate with each other, sharing. Natia found a young boy who had become an orphan after his parents went missing in the woods, to share her bowl of food with. Aiyana sat on Red Bear's lap as she fed him from their bowl of food and I stood there looking at the joy of happiness and love between all these people, forgetting to share my food with a partner. A hand reached into the bowl I was holding and picked up some rice and meat and guided it toward my mouth. I looked up to my right to see my guardian angel, my protector.

"May the gods forever bless you. Happy Thanksgiving, Elu," Tate said as his lips created half a smile.

I ate from Tate's hands and he ate from mine. The village was filled with happiness, love, and joy. This was by far one of the most incredible experiences of my life. After we all finished feasting, the children ran toward Red Bear.

"My brave cubs, go out to become one with the shadows and when the fire begins to die down, the sons of Achomawi, as well as our guests, the she-wolf, and Apisi, will begin to hunt until we have only one Molimo," Red Bear shouted.

The children ran to their parents, kissed their mothers and then got picked up by their fathers. They rubbed their fathers' faces and then rubbed their face for good luck. They were as young as five years old. Natia's little orphan boy, who had shared food with her, pulled on her dress. She bent down to give him a kiss and then he ran back toward Red Bear. He raised his hands to be picked up and Red Bear picked him up and he placed both his little hands on Red Bears cheeks then on his cheeks, then Red Bear let him down and off he went.

Not long after, the fire began to die down. All the parents of the children sat beside the fire and waited for their children to return.

"Natia, are you ready?" Aiyana said.

"Yeah, let's do it," Natia replied.

Before my eyes, Natia and Aiyana, as well as other tribeswomen, transformed into their natural forms. Natia became this graceful bronze-colored wolf. As she turned and walked over to me, I smiled. She brushed her head into my stomach. Aiyana and the tribeswomen transformed into big, brave bears; Aiyana had a very light-brown fur that caught the light of the moon and reflected the glare off her. The tribeswomen and Natia ran off into the woods to find the children. It was exciting to watch and soon it would be exciting to take part. Natia found two little girls who rode on top of her back and a young boy who hung from her mouth by his clothing. When she returned they ran off to see their parents. The tribeswomen brought back several children that were giggling away, and then Aiyana came back.

"Apisi, there is only one child to be found. Will you help us?" Aiyana said.

"Sure, let's go get Molimo!" I replied.

"El, the last child is Enyeto, the orphan child," Natia said to me telepathically.

"How did you do that?" I said to her.

"Wolves can't speak so we communicate through each other's minds," she said.

As I made my way through the forest to find Enyeto, I began to get deeper and deeper. I approached a big rock between two big trees and I heard a little giggle.

"I wonder where Enyeto could be," I said out loud. "He's not on this tree or behind that one...I wonder about this big rock?" I added.

I peeped over the rock and he wasn't there. I frowned at the sight of him not being there as I had just heard a giggle; I rushed around the rock, looking all around it. Then, not too far away, I could see a mountain lion approaching Enyeto and him walking toward it.

"Enyeto! Stop!" I shouted.

I ran over toward Enyeto and the mountain lion. As I came close to Enyeto, I pulled him away from the mountain lion's reach and it swung its paws in a vicious attack toward me. As I shielded Enyeto, I felt my body shaking. The mountain lion slowly walked toward us and as I backed away, it roared at us and there and then, out of nowhere, I growled and then barked at the mountain lion. As we had our standoff, I had no control of my body. As I stepped toward the mountain lion, it backed off and then I barked again and it ran. I looked back at Enyeto and he was so frightened by what had just happened I had to pick him up and put him on my back. We made our way toward the village with me carrying him.

"Enyeto, are you OK?" I said.

He didn't reply.

NATIVE - ⏋⏌F 106

"It's OK. These things happen. You have to be brave though, you're now Molimo." I turned my head to see if he was OK.

"I'm Molimo?" Enyeto said.

"Yeah. You were the hardest to find. You were the last one," I replied.

He smiled and hugged my back tighter.

"Do you think She-wolf and Red Bear will praise me, Apisi?" he said.

"Of course they will, Enyeto, but you can't tell anyone about the mountain lion because they aren't as brave as you, so you might make them scared because they're not Molimo. Our secret, OK?"

"OK, Apisi," he replied.

We got back to the village and the tribeswomen and men greeted Enyeto and applauded him on his new title of Molimo and for winning the game. He ran over to Natia and hugged her. He then ran over to Red Bear and put the palm of his little hand on Red Bear's forehead as he bent down to greet him. Tate walked over to me.

"Tate, I need to tell you something." I walked toward a quieter part of the village.

"Back when I was looking for Enyeto, we came across a mountain lion that tried to attack us. Out of nowhere, I growled and then barked at him. I could feel my body starting to change."

"El, you need to be careful. It's getting closer."

"I know, I know…The mountain lion…it was like it knew who I was once I growled and barked."

"Mountain lions are known to be ferocious creatures and they prey on the weak. Be very careful, Elu. They come from a tribe that isn't so trustworthy."

"So there's a tribe of them?"

"Not quite. Mountain lions are solitary animals. They like to do things individually but they do have partners and cubs to look after. I will bring this forth to Red Bear and let him know what has happened without alarming anyone."

"OK," I said as my eyes paced back and forth, thinking about what had just happened.

"Elu, you did well; don't worry."

As the evening went on, the men joked and laughed between themselves, the women put the children to sleep, and Natia placed Enyeto in Red Bear's house to sleep. I sat staring into the fire and thinking about the trip.

"Apisi, are you OK?" Red Bear came and sat aside me.

"Yeah, there's just so much to know, to learn, to become. I don't know how to take it all in," I replied.

"And you will. These things take time. Just let your

mind, body, and soul grow, day by day, go with your natural feelings, and you will always be in the right place."

"Thanks, Red Bear."

"There's no need for thanks, Apisi. You are the one we have all been waiting for. We owe many thanks to you and those before you."

The next morning, Tate was awake before Natia and me. He was putting all of our stuff in the back of the truck as I walked toward him. Red Bear and Aiyana were talking to him.

"Ready to go, El?" Tate said.

"Yeah. Red Bear, Aiyana, thank you for welcoming us into your home, feeding us, and treating us as one of your own," I said as I hugged Aiyana and then shook Red Bear's hand.

"Apisi, you are welcome into our home anytime you wish. May the gods bless you and those with you," Aiyana said.

"I think your friend isn't too keen on leaving just yet," Red Bear said as he looked into the direction of Natia.

Natia was kneeling down and hugging Enyeto. She let go of him and kissed him on his forehead.

"Be brave, my Molimo. I will come back to visit you soon." Natia said holding back tears.

She walked over toward us and thanked Red Bear
and Aiyana. We all got into the truck and made our
way back to Los Angeles. Natia was still sad from
leaving Enyeto and the Achomawi tribe, so I placed
my arm around her and comforted her, as I rested
my face on her head.

"So, didn't I say it would be great?" Tate said.

"Yeah, it was an amazing experience and I'd love to
visit the Achomawi again," I replied.

Tate drove as far as Fresno and then I forced him to
pull over and let me drive so he could get some rest.
Tate fell asleep on Natia's lap as she was fast asleep
against the window; when I had pulled-over for a
break, I grabbed my cell phone and took a picture.
As I drove the rest of the way back to our apartment,
I couldn't help but think about this Saturday; USC
vs. UCLA and me finally confronting Number 28. I
know Natia had said that my feeling like this about
him was my heart telling me he was my soul mate
but I didn't want to believe that because I should be
with Tate. The way he looked at me, the way he
talked to me, and the way he was always there for
me showed me he was perfect, but Number 28 had
stolen my heart before Tate had the chance to. I
wondered if he felt the same way about me and
whether he'd felt the same feelings when he'd first
seen me.

Natia mentioned that if he didn't feel the same way I
felt about him, it could be very painful for me as my
heart and soul were giving him my all, so for him to
reject it, it would leave my soul and heart in

complete devastation and sorrow. All I knew was
that no matter what happened, it was written for me
and that it would pan out.

Friday morning arrived and it was Thanksgiving Day, so while Natia was asleep I headed down to the coffee shop to grab us our daily addiction. I thought it would be nice for Tate, Natia, and me to have an American Thanksgiving dinner, so I booked a table for us at 21 Oceanfront opposite Newport Beach. In the evening we would catch a taxi down there; I just needed to get hold of Tate. As I walked back into our room, I woke Natia by opening the door; with her arms spread wide open and her long big yawn, she said, "Hey, El, is that coffee I smell?"

"Sure is." I sat on her bed. "Don't plan anything for tonight, I've got a surprise for you," I added.

"Oh really, what's that?" Natia replied as she sipped on her coffee.

"I can't tell you otherwise it wouldn't be a surprise. I can tell you one thing though."

"Go on…"

"We both need new dresses!"

"Shopping!" Natia shouted.

I wasn't the type of girly girl to go shopping every weekend and all my possessions weren't pink. I preferred the simple, sophisticated things, but I knew this would make Natia happy after leaving Enyeto yesterday. We took the bus to Westfield Shopping Center in Santa Monica and shopped around all day. It was quite relaxing and nice for a change. As we walked back toward the bus stop, Tate surprised us from behind. He placed his hands on both of our shoulders and walked right between us.

"Ladies," he greeted us.

"Oh my God, you scared me there, Tate," Natia said.

"Dude, you need to get a cell phone. I've been trying to get hold of you all day," I said to Tate.

"Ah...I didn't notice you needed me. Just caw next time you need me." He laughed.

"Oh yeah, like I'm going to do that. How am I even supposed to do that?" I replied.

"Easy, you just go..." and he cawed. "Now, you try," he added.

"What? That's ridiculous. I can't do that!"

"Try!" he persisted.

So I tried cawing. I made a very silly noise and embarrassed myself. Natia and Tate laughed at me.

"What are you doing? Everyone knows coyotes can't caw," Tate mocked me.

"What? But you said..." I replied.

"Here, I got this for you." He handed me a plastic, tube-shaped item that had some sort of whistle attached to it.

"What is it?"

"It's a crow caller, so anytime you do need me, just

blow into it and I'll come."

"So you made me try cawing for no reason?"

"Well, not 'no reason.' It was funny." He laughed.

"What the hell." I punched him on his arm and we all laughed.

"So listen, Tate, I've got a surprise for you and Natia tonight. Can I trust you to dress smart?" I said.

"What's wrong with this?" He looked down at his clothes.

"No way! Get a nice shirt, some trousers, and shoes. Natia and I would gladly help you if you want."

"Yeah, Tate, let's go find you something smart," Natia added.

"Actually, you know what? I'll go get that right now. You two carry on. I can manage." He jogged off in the other direction.

"Don't be late!" I shouted back at him.

We caught the bus back home and got ready for the evening. Natia wore a beautiful red dress that would break necks instantly. She was so gorgeous but yet so humble. She didn't realize how pretty she really was.

"Nat, you look amazing. Let me take a picture. You can send it to your parents later." I snapped a picture on my phone.

"Here, El, let me take one of you too." I wore a navy blue dress similar to Natia's. It was simple but Natia kept complimenting me on how pretty I apparently looked.

I passed my phone to Natia so she could take a picture of me; she took a few and then browsed through the pictures to show me.

"Hold on! What's this?" Natia shoved the phone in my face. It was the picture of Tate sleeping on her. I laughed.

"That was on the way back home yesterday. Look how cute you two are." We laughed.

We went outside to hail a cab. When none of them decided they wanted to stop, we walked a bit further down the road and then one taxi pulled up by us and the passenger window rolled down.

"Evening ladies," Tate said.

He looked so handsome. He had his hair tied back and shaped up all neat. He wore a smart white shirt with gray trousers.

"You scrub up well, don't you Tate?" Natia said.

"Well I've got to look my best if I'm to take you two beautiful ladies out," he replied.

Tate was such a gentleman. He paid for the taxi and refused to take any cash from us. He then went on to open the door for us and closed it behind us. We all stood outside the restaurant and I walked toward the entrance as Natia and Tate followed me in.

"Good evening, do you have reservations?" the man at the front desk of the restaurant said.

"Yes, it's under Miss Black," I replied. The front of house scuffed through some papers.

"Ah...yes, Miss Black plus two. If you would like to follow me this way, I will show you where your table is."

We followed him to our table. Tate pulled our chairs out for us before we could sit down.

"So this is the big surprise, hey, El?" Natia said.

"Yeah, I figured it's Thanksgiving and there are two very special people I would like to share it with. Don't get me wrong, I loved our experience with the Achomawi tribe, but I wanted us to do something together, just the three of us," I replied.

"It's a very nice gesture, El. Thank you," Tate said.

"It is, Elu. Thank you." Natia smiled.

We went on to eat and dine at this really nice restaurant, joking and laughing, and having a memorable Thanksgiving evening. After we left the restaurant, Tate linked his arms with me and Natia and he led us to the beach across the road.

"Where are we going, Tate?" I asked.

"Well, Miss Black, you treated us to a very nice

Thanksgiving meal so I want to share something with both of you to add to this amazing night," he replied.

"Hope you don't plan on skinny dipping because I'm too full right now to be running into the ocean naked." Natia laughed.

"No, of course not. Right, let's take a seat here and just lie back and look up at the sky."

As we all sat down and lay back into the sand, the sky was pitch black with the stars illuminating its beauty.

"It's beautiful, Tate," I said. I placed my fingers in between his hand, as the three of us lay there gazing into the wonder of the stars.

"Every night I find a peaceful place where I can go and appreciate the stories, the guidance, and the beauty of the stars. If everyone took a bit of time out every day to appreciate the natural beauty of the world, we would all live in a better place today," Tate said as he lost himself in the night sky.

"They are, Tate. They are amazing…" I replied.

"You see that one? The brightest one in the sky? That one's the North Star…I never met my parents but whenever I used to ask my auntie back home about my mother, she would always say, if you look into the sky in the darkness of the night, your mother was like the brightest star in a world full of darkness," Tate said.

"I'm sorry to hear that, Tate…What about your father?" Natia replied. I gripped Tate's hand a little tighter.

"Ahh…I'd rather not talk about him." Tate went silent.

"I'm sure your mother was an amazing person. She had to be for you to be her son. She would be proud of you, Tate," I said.

We gazed into the sky, appreciating the beauty of the stars. I couldn't stop looking at the North Star; at how beautiful and bright it was. It outshone all the other stars. It truly was the one star that stood out from the rest.

"So, this Thanksgiving, you guys both shared with me something that is special for you. I would like to do the same," Natia said.

Tate and I sat up.

"Sure, what's that, Nat?" I asked.

"Since we're all doing things together for the first time, I don't believe we've all had a drink together," she replied.

"Oh…I don't know. I'm not really a drinker…Plus you guys aren't even twenty-one yet!" Tate replied.

"Come on, Tate. Don't be boring," Natia said.

"She does have a point," I added.

Natia pushed her bottom lip out and gave Tate her puppy dog eyes. I laughed and stood up as I pulled Tate's arm.

"OK, one drink…" He gave in.

We strolled down the street to the nearest bar; Natia wasted no time and ordered us a shot each. We sat at the bar laughing and joking as I looked back at Tate. He looked so confused and uncomfortable.

"That's one small drink, Nat," Tate said.

She laughed and pulled in close to Tate.

"Have you ever had a drink before?" she whispered.

"Yeah! Yeah, of course, I have." He stuck his chest out with pride.

"Go on then…" Natia persisted.

"Tate…Wait…" I tried to stop him.

Tate lifted his glass up and knocked back his shot. His expression went from macho to 'Get me some water!' in a matter of seconds.

"Wow, that's strong!" He squirmed.

"Nat, you're such a bad influence," I said to her.

"What? It's good for the soul!" She laughed and knocked back her shot.

"OK, I think I'll just stick to something a bit less

potent," Tate said.

We carried on drinking through the night being playful and chucking snacks from the bar at one and another. By now I was a bit tipsy and so was Tate, but Natia was absolutely drunk.

"Nat, come on, let's get you home. You've had one too many," I said as she raised her drink to her mouth.

"Yeah, let's get you both home," Tate said.

Natia stood up with my assistance but as she stood up she lost the grip on her glass and dropped it, causing it to smash on the bar.

"Elu, your purse." Tate picked my purse up from the bar before it got all wet but in doing so, he cut the palm of his hand on some glass. "Ah!" He pulled his hand back.

The sudden accident seemed to make us all snap out of our drunken behavior. I rushed over to see if Tate was OK and placed my hands under his. Natia called over to the bartender to get a cloth and clean up the glass.

"Tate, are you OK?" I panicked.

"Yeah, yeah, I'm fine. I just caught my hand on a bit of glass." As he opened his palm out for me to see, the blood made its way onto my hands. My heart began to race and the craving and lust for the sight of blood before me made me feel aroused. The smell made me weak but at the same time gave me a strong urge. Tate stared at me completely worried, as he knew what I was sensing and feeling.

"ELU!" he shouted.

He grabbed the cloth off of the bartender and wrapped it around his hand and then he approached me, staring at my hands. He grabbed them both, rubbing the blood off of them. Only then did I slowly begin to calm down. My heart started easing its pace and my urges and senses slowly faded from this animalistic feeling.

"It's fine, Tate. I can manage," I said as I tried to stop him rubbing my hands.

"No! Don't worry, I got this!" He continued rubbing the cloth into my hands.

"Tate, stop!" I pulled my hands away.

A stranger from the bar came over and pulled Tate's shoulder.

"I think that's enough, son," the stranger said.

My heart started racing again.

"Let go of him!" I launched the stranger off of Tate and sent him flying over to the other side of the bar.

I stared at this stranger in complete shock at what I had just done but the feeling of doing something wrong felt good. It was a dark temptation lurking around me to persist in hurting this man some more because he'd put his hands on Tate. I stepped toward the stranger and then I heard my name.

"Elu!" Natia shouted.

I turned around and Natia placed both of her hands on my face.

"Elu! Stop! Focus on me!" She tried calming me down.

"Girls, you're going to have to leave, please!" the bartender shouted.

Natia placed her arms around me and assisted me out of the bar this time. I was still in shock at the feeling I had just had.

"El, it's fine. You're going to be just fine," Natia kept reassuring me.

"Wait! Where's Tate? Tate!" I shouted.

"El, stop. He's gone," she replied.

"Where?"

"I don't know, but we need to get you home."

We drove back to the apartment. Natia and I both sat in the back seat. She didn't let go of me for the whole ride. I eventually fell asleep from all of the adrenaline that had surged through my body; I was now crashing.

The next day I woke up and everything from the previous night seemed like such a blur, but it wasn't from the alcohol; it was from what had happened. I felt weak and drained from the whole situation at the bar. It took a lot out of me. Natia had already been up and out of the apartment. She must have gone to get our coffee, or so I was hoping. The door opened and in came Natia.

"Elu, you're up. How are you feeling?" she asked.

"Um...tired, to say the least. What happened last night?" I replied.

"Don't you remember?"

"Yeah...But it happened so quickly, I can only remember brief parts."

"You just flipped. Tate cut his hand on some glass I accidently dropped and then some guy came over, and you literally threw him across the bar. When I called you over it was like you were possessed." She paused.

"Possessed? What do you mean? How?"

"It's hard to say. It was like something took over you...Don't you remember that part?"

"Yeah, I remember..." As Natia jogged my memory, I started to remember the feeling of a lustful temptation for everything; the warm thick blood that had occupied the palms of my hands, the sweet smell that lingered through my nose, and bedded the imaginative taste on my tongue.

"EL!" Natia shouted. "What you thinking?"

"I...Nat...Is it possible? Nah...It can't be..." I tried making sense of my situation.

"What is it, Elu?" she replied.

I've never desired blood in any way, shape, or form before but last night wasn't anything I had ever felt previously. It wasn't my natural animal instincts of the Coyote; this was different. This was me, yearning for blood.

"Seriously, El...Where do you go? You just drift off in the middle of conversations all the time," Natia said.

"I need to talk to Tate," I replied.

"Oh..."

"Nat, it's not that I'm hiding something but I just don't know how or what that was and I think Tate does," I lied. I knew exactly what it was but I just didn't know how it was possible.

"It's fine, Elu. I know it's all still a lot to take in."

"Oh, here's your coffee by the way." She handed me a warm cup of coffee.

"Thanks, Nat... You never seem freaked out by these things that happen. Why is that?" I said as I leaned back onto the wall.

"I guess when you're brought up with these things

being the norm, it doesn't surprise you. Listen, El, you really need to be careful. Try your best to keep your feelings and emotions controlled. Last night at the bar, if you had changed you could have hurt a lot of people," she said in a worried tone while looking down at her coffee.

I knew it had nothing to do with me turning into the coyote, nothing at all. It was something else.

"I know, Nat. I'll try my hardest. It just springs up on you though, doesn't it?" I played on what she had said.

"Just keep trying. Hey, so tomorrow is the big day! UCLA, Number 28? What are you going to say? What are you going to do? What's the plan? Tell me." She interrogated me; she came across the room and sat on my bed with her legs crossed, waiting for me to give her the game plan.

"I know...like I don't have enough going on as it is. Um... well, I figured I'd try and catch him outside the locker rooms on his way out and just talk to him and explain myself and how I'm feeling. That's it. That's all I've got so far."

"That's fine, Elu! That's all you need. If it's meant to be, it will happen. Trust your heart."

"Thanks, Nat...I need to find Tate."

"Well, have fun with that. I've got plenty of rehearsing all day and all night by the looks of it."

I got ready for my day; grabbed everything I needed,

including Tate's crow caller, and headed up to Silver Lake Reservoir. It was a peaceful area where a lot of students went to study and enjoy nature, so I figured I'd take my sketchbook too and see if I could get some work done.

As I arrived, there were a few students scattered around. I found a nice spot overlooking the reservoir, where I sat down and pulled out my sketchbook. The crow caller rolled out with it. I needed to speak to Tate, it reminded me. I blew into the crow caller twice. As it cawed, I looked around to see if Tate was anywhere in sight. I couldn't see him. I opened up my sketchbook and sharpened my pencils while looking over the reservoir. I began drawing in the meantime.

"Hey," Tate said as he came out of nowhere and sat down alongside me.

"Decided to show then?" I replied.

"Was in the neighborhood. No biggie."

"So…" I paused.

"So."

"Last night." I paused again.

"Yup, last night," he replied. "You know what that was, don't you?" he added.

"Yeah…So what does this mean, Tate? I'm confused. I thought I was the heir of The Great Coyote?" I put my sketchbook aside and gave Tate my full attention.

"You are, Elu…But you're a hybrid. You possess both traits and abilities of The Great Coyote and the immortals," he said as he looked down at the floor.

"But how? How is this possible, Tate? I don't understand. I thought I was on the good side?" I began to panic.

"Elu…it's not about us vs. them. It's about standing up for what's right and protecting the people we love and who are innocent. I don't know how it's possible but it doesn't change the fact that you're still the heir to The Great Coyote."

"So does this mean I will have to drink blood?" I replied.

"No." He laughed. "Of course not. You're a hybrid. That means you have the powers and abilities of both coyote and immortal."

"But what about these urges and uncontrollable feelings that creep up on me. How do I tame them?"

"Time, Elu, just give it time. You will be able to," he replied.

"Great…Time…We've got plenty of that to spare. So what do we do now?"

"Well, when you have your first transformation, everything will just fall into place. You will feel, see, and do things that the genes you've inherited allow you to do. But until then you're just going to have to hold on. I'm always watching over you, Elu. Don't worry about being alone because I'll be there forever." Tate held my hand and pulled me in closer for a hug. I just embraced the moment and trusted his guidance.

So now that things were even more complicated, the breakdown was; I had college to worry about, my family couldn't know any of this because I'd most likely put their life in danger, I was the heir to The Great Coyote, but technically I was a hybrid. Even though I was half-coyote, half-immortal, I was currently none of these things because I hadn't fully gained my abilities. I was trapped in my human body, which by the way was run down, tired, and forever hungry; plus the fact that I really liked Tate but I couldn't ever be with him because my heart and my desires belonged to Number 28. To top it all off, I couldn't seem to finish this damn drawing.

Tate flew off after a while. He knew I had quite a bit of college work to catch up on so he left me to it. I began drawing the reservoir, the trees and people, but after several attempts of sharpening my pencil and failing to get the right shade of the water, I called it a day and decided to find somewhere to eat. I hadn't eaten since morning; well, if you call coffee food. I began walking to find somewhere to eat and then...

"Hey Elu! Wait! Hold on!" it was Jason.

"What?" I asked as I clutched on to my bag.

"Wow! What's with the attitude? Aren't we

friends?" he replied.

"Friends? Friends?! Your team mate physically harassed me and probably would have carried on if my friend hadn't come and helped me," I said to him in an aggressive tone as I stopped walking.

"Wait, that had nothing to with me, Elu. If anything, I stopped it," he pleaded.

Tate flew down in his crow form by us and cawed at Jason.

"Damn, that's one big-ass bird. Go away!" he said to Tate.

"You know, I'd be very careful about how you treat crows, because they don't forget faces. It's a fact." I smiled sarcastically.

"Yeah...Um, well, listen, I'm about to get something to eat. Like, if you wanted to, if you fancied it, I don't know, if you were hungry?" he stuttered.

He was clearly nervous and, bless him, I could tell he was trying, plus I was starving.

"Yes Jason, I'm starving. Food would be great right now." I looked back at Tate and winked to say it was OK.

"Cool...Cool...Um well, it can be my way of making it up to you for the other night; on me," he said as he brushed his hands through his hair.

"On you?" I replied.

"On me." He smiled.

"OK, cool."

We headed down the road to the Astro Family Restaurant about twenty minutes from the lake.

"So your friend the other night; is that like your boyfriend or something?" Jason asked.

"Who, Tate? Nah, he's like my older brother," I replied.

"Oh…older brother. You know, he tore the tendons in Royce's hand?"

"Maybe Royce shouldn't have tried attacking him with a bottle," I replied sarcastically.

"Maybe…"

"What did Adam say about the whole situation?"

"He didn't, to be honest. He kept quiet afterward and didn't really talk that much the next day either."

"What happened? Did his ego get damaged along with his pretty face?" I persisted, taking digs at Jason.

"Yeah, he had to have four stitches on the side of his face from crashing through that window."

I smirked. We entered the restaurant and took a seat at the bar. As we browsed through the menu, I could tell Jason felt bad about that night, so it was a bit of a jerk move to keep on at him when realistically he didn't do anything but stop the fight.

"But anyway, that's behind us. Posed naked for any more classes lately, Jason?" I laughed as I looked at the menu.

"No...Just the one off. You been punching any more football players?" he laughed.

The waitress walked over and asked for our orders.

"Hi guys, welcome to Astro. What can I get you?" she said.

"I'll have the steak sandwich, rare, please," Jason replied.

"Can I have the fried chicken, fries, and loads of coleslaw, please?" I replied.

"Big appetite?" Jason said.

"Breakfast and lunch, right now. Girl got to eat!" I laughed.

"And what drinks can I get you guys?" the waitress asked.

"I'll have an orange juice, please," Jason said.

"Me too," I replied.

The waitress went off and we both sat there for a solid five minutes in awkward silence.

"So…" Jason said.

"So…" I replied as I sipped on my orange juice.

"Hey, I know what, actually!" I blurted out.

"What's that?" Jason replied.

"Number 28 from UCLA; what can you tell me about him?"

"Number 28, are you serious? What can't I tell you about him is the question."

"Well?" I waited for an answer.

"Duane Toa is the leading scorer of all time. His high score broke the record last year. Every college in the country wanted him. He was all over the news and media. How did you not see him?" Jason said enthusiastically.

"Oh, I did see him…But what else do you know about him?" We both began eating our food.

"Well, he's one hell of an athlete, I'll tell you that much. Um… there was this thing in the news that kind of made him even more likable. He was left on someone's doorstep as a child and ever since he started playing football he just got so much attention that the story eventually came out. He's been the number one prospect before he even reached his last year of high school. There's no doubt that every team in the pro league will want him, come the end of his college years. Why do you ask anyway?"

"Um…no reason, I just thought that's where I knew him from," I stuttered.

"Hey, well, we're playing them tomorrow. You should come watch. Hopefully we can take the 'W' this time."

"Yeah, no, of course, I'll be there."

"Cool. Well, I need to get to practice. Do you need a ride or you cool?" He got up to pay the bill.

"Nah, I'm fine. Thank you, Jason. Thanks for the meal," I replied.

"Ah…No worries. Good catching up with you, Elu. Tomorrow?"

"Yeah, tomorrow. See you then."

"See ya!" he shouted as he went through the doors.

"Duane Toa," I said to myself. Well, at least I had a name now. I just hoped it would all go well tomorrow. I needed something good to hold on to right now, but how would I explain what I am to him? Surely, if he felt the way I felt about him, he would understand. The thought of him gave me butterflies and made me feel warm. I hoped he'd be able to say the same about me; otherwise this wasn't going to go down well. I left the restaurant and caught the bus back to the apartment. It was pretty late in the evening and Natia still hadn't come home. I thought I'd have a shower and get an early night for tomorrow's big day.

But I was so wrong. The excitement and the thought of the possibilities kept me awake and it wasn't the usual time I went to sleep, so I was wide awake. Natia still wasn't home, so it wasn't even as if I could speak to her. I put some trainers on and a long white top and headed down toward Tommy Trojan. I thought I'd spend some time with him and see if I could finish off this drawing of Tate.

I began walking down toward Tommy Trojan. It wasn't a long walk, about ten minutes, but as I passed Cromwell Field, there it was again; that feeling of my body feeling abnormal. Gravity was pulling me in the direction of Tommy Trojan; all my focus was on getting to the statue as fast as I could. As I ran, the feeling became more intense and magnified the closer I came. As I gained a view of Tommy Trojan, I saw he wasn't alone. There were three guys dressed in black, painting the statue yellow and blue. They had to be football players from UCLA. Natia had told me they always tried attacking the statue on nights before the game.

"Hey! Stop!" I shouted at the three black figures.

The three of them jumped off the statue and two of them began running. The other just stood there staring at me. I couldn't see who it was because his face was covered, but this feeling I had kept growing. I felt so aroused and uncontrollably in lust.

"D! What are you doing? Let's go!" one of the guys shouted as they ran off.

This tall, broad, and built guy stood before me

dressed all in black. With his face covered, he looked like he was ready to rob a bank. I approached him one step at a time, making my body feel warmer and lighter. The danger standing before me was as real as it could get, but it wasn't dangerous for me as I knew exactly who it was. I stood about an inch away from him and I looked up at him. As I stood under his face, he looked down at me and slowly lifted the bottom of his balaclava, revealing his mouth and whispering, "You...You're the one that's making me feel like this?"

I didn't think, I just threw myself at him and wrapped my arms around him, tightening and squeezing into his body. I rested my head on his chest and I could feel his heart smashing against it. The vibration and sound echoed into my ear and down into my body as it soothed my heart. He placed his head down toward mine. I could feel his breath sweeping the hair on my head and as I looked up into his half-revealed face I loosened my arms from around his waist and placed both of my hands on his face. He tilted his head toward mine. I could feel my soul lifting and yearning to be with his. I slowly caressed his lips with mine as we kissed. It was my first ever kiss. I pulled off his balaclava as we carried on kissing. We were both lost in the moment and in the presence of each other; nothing else mattered in the world but us.

As we detached ourselves from each other, I looked up at Duane as he looked down at me. The feelings were so intimate. His long shadowy hair rested on his broad shoulders and his cool gray eyes didn't move from mine.

"We need to get away from here. Campus security will be here any minute!" I grabbed Duane's hand and ran to the other side of the Alumni Park.

We stood there face to face. To him, I was this complete stranger that he had just met, and to me he was the boy that had stolen my heart. He was the one my soul had been looking for since the beginning of my existence.

"Duane...I—" I started to mumble.

"Before you say anything, what was that? What is this feeling?" he said in his deep voice.

"I...I don't know where to begin..." I mumbled on.

"How about with your name?" He laughed.

I smiled and placed my hand on his chest as I looked up at him.

"My name's Elu. I go to USC. I'm from a cold, rainy town up north, and...I've had this crazy strange feeling about you ever since I saw you at the first pre-season game."

"You were at the game? You were in the stands?" He stepped forward placing his hands on my waist and bringing me closer to him.

"Yeah...I was..."

"I felt it. I could feel my body going really warm from head to toe; literally every single part of my body. I thought it might have just been from playing in the heat, but then my body felt light, like really light. My heart felt as if it was leaving my body and gravity left me from every direction except toward the stands. As it pulled me toward there, I needed to get off the pitch. I didn't know what it was so I ran back to the locker rooms."

"I know, Duane…Listen, I need to tell you something."

Duane's face suddenly changed. He looked angry. His jaw clenched and he let go of my waist and began making noises out of pain. He started to moan and scream. I didn't know what was wrong with him.

"GET AWAY! GET AWAY!" He screamed.

"Duane!" I shouted.

"GO! NOW!" His voice trembled in agony.

He fell to one knee as he raised his hand up to me to not come any closer. My heart began hammering so fast that my body began to heat up and I could feel a tingling sensation harnessing around me. The sky started to dye into dark red colors and the moon became tinted. The sky looked as if it had filled with blood. I remembered hearing about this from the story Natia had told me; 'My blood will flow through its veins, causing Ao-Toto and you will no longer have a hold over me,' and Ao-Toto meant Cloud of Blood, but then this meant that Duane was bloodline related to Malietoa Ula'.

Duane stood up and walked straight over to me, but

it wasn't him. He had turned into something else. He grabbed me around my arms with a very firm grip and as I looked up into his eyes they had turned blood red.

"Duane, let go. You're hurting me!"

He didn't say anything. He just kept squeezing, his jaw clenched and his teeth gritted. He looked like he was trying to fight it back, but he was squeezing me around my arms too hard now; I started shaking.

I began to shake uncontrollably. I felt my bone structure begin to alter and reform and fur began to shoot through my skin. I had fully transfigured into the coyote, but as I did, in a sudden escape to be released from Duane's grip, I threw my claws out, cutting into Duane's chest. I stood before Duane as a coyote and he stood before me as an immortal. He looked down at his chest to where I'd left scratch marks and he ran. I tried to run after him but he was too fast and my body was still sore from turning. There was no way I could keep up with him. As I howled and cried for him, he ran out of sight and was gone into the dark night, which was filled with blood and sorrow.

I couldn't let anyone see me like this and I didn't want to go back to the apartment. I needed to be alone. I needed to be able to take this in by myself. I hit most parts of the back alleys through L.A. and hid in the shadows until the streets were clear; then I made my way to the Angeles National Forest. It was safe; there weren't any people about so I ran through the fields until I came across some tall trees where I could rest.

My heart was gone. All love lost. What had I done? Duane and I had been there together, everything was perfect, and then he just changed out of nowhere. Where did he go? Was he going to be OK? Was he still alive? These questions kept playing back and forth through my mind. I had just lost the first person I had ever loved. I'd always thought about who my first love would be. Whether he would be with me for the rest of my life, what our kids would look like, and what our life would turn out to be like, but none of those questions meant anything now. I howled and cried the heartache from my body into the red skies and moped around the trees, waiting for Duane to maybe hear me...But he didn't and he wasn't coming back.

I sat by a tree with the moon in sight. As the red tint from the clouds began to fade away, a bright star pierced through the sky and lit up the dark ceiling. It was the North Star and it reminded me of Tate. Where was he? Why wasn't he there to protect me or guide me? On this night, my first night as a coyote, and my first night meeting my life partner, I cried myself to sleep. There I lay, as the stars watched over me and the moon kept the darkness away.

The next morning I woke up to the bright sun's rays
peeking onto my fur and warming me up. I yawned,
making a funny noise. I had forgotten I was still a
coyote. It didn't feel weird. Surprisingly, it felt
natural. I stood on all fours and walked around for a
bit until I was a little more awake. I could hear the
splashing of water. There had to be a source of water
nearby so I ran in that direction. As I came closer, I
saw that it was a waterfall. No one was in sight so I
approached the water with caution. As I panted with
my tongue hanging from my mouth, I looked down
at the water to drink and I could see my reflection. I
had radiant shining white fur that came down the
middle of my head, down my nose, and on either
side of my face. Covering my eyes and ears was
silver gray fur. My tail was also silver gray with a
white tip at the end; I looked like something not of
this world. I was in complete awe. After admiring
my coyote fur, I plunged my head into the water,
gulping it in big amounts as it filled my thirst but it
didn't sustain my hunger. I needed meat; something
raw. The thought made me slightly disgusted but it
was what my body craved. I noticed rabbit
droppings near the waterfall so I began my hunt,
sniffing out and tracking down my prey. It wasn't
long before I closed in on a nice fluffy gray rabbit. I
clutched onto its neck and squeezed the life out of it.
I then began to feast.

After breakfast, I carried on exploring the forest and
the many earthly features it had to offer. I liked
being in my coyote form; it was a new way of
escaping from everyone else and being one with
nature; but as much as this beautiful place kept me at
ease, the heartache never left. Shoots of pains ran

through my body as if it was missing an organ. It made me howl and cry. It was the only way of expressing my pain. As the day went by and sunset slowly approached, I came across some rocks. I walked past and through and then out of nowhere, there was one of them again. I growled and barked at the enemy as he slowly started to approach me.

"I'm not here to hurt you," the mountain lion communicated with me.

"What do you want?" I replied.

"You are Apisi. We have all been waiting for you."

"Who's we and how do I know I can trust you? I came across one of your kind back in Pit River and you tried attacking me, as well as an infant."

"Apisi, there are many different tribes. I am from the tribe of Jaega in Palm Beach, Florida. My name is Iye."

"What are you doing here in Los Angeles, Iye?" I replied.

"I am seeking help from the other tribes. The Red Indians are becoming more of a threat and problem in Palm Beach."

"I'm sorry to hear that, but I can be of no help right now as I have a lot to handle."

"I know this, Apisi. The truth is not written; the truth is in our hearts, the knowledge in our heads, the beast is in our body. Tame the beast and all will become clear." Iye turned around and began to walk off.

"Wait! What did you just say?" I remembered hearing that somewhere but I couldn't remember where.

"The truth is not written; the truth is in our hearts, the knowledge in our heads, the beast is in our body. Tame the beast and all will become clear…Everyone knows these words, Apisi," he replied. I still couldn't remember where I'd heard that before.

"Iye, do you know of any good Red Indians?"

"Many, Apisi. There are the ones that want to live in peace just as much as we do."

"Where can I find them, Iye? Here in L.A., where would you go if you wanted to find them?"

"Apisi, seek knowledge and it will come before you, but be careful who you trust. I must go, until another day Apisi, farewell." Iye left sprinting across the mountains.

"What? Wait!" I pleaded.

I didn't know where to go or who I could trust. I needed to see Duane but he could be anywhere and I didn't have a clue where to start.

I carried on walking and sprinting through the woods and hills getting used to my coyote form. The feeling was great. My fur kept me warm, I didn't become as hungry as I often did, and my thirst was also preserved to a minimum. But the way I could run and jump gave me a new sense of adventure. My senses were heightened to be able to smell things from a further distance, hear things from afar, and I was aware when trouble or danger was nearby. I liked being a coyote. It made so much sense to me. I was free, the truth was in my heart, the knowledge in my mind, and I had controlled the beast. I had grown and understood my natives.

As I rested under a large tree, keeping out of sight of the lurking moonlight, I heard cawing. I raised my head and my snout to the sky; I could see a black bird flying around above the trees. It was Tate. I was so glad to see him. He flew down toward me, transforming into his human form as he landed. I stood and walked over to him as he began to walk toward me.

"Elu...I'm so sorry." He hugged my head into his chest as he rubbed his hands through my fur.

"Elu!" I heard a voice communicate with me.

I turned around and saw Natia running through the woods in her wolf form. I began sprinting toward her. As we came closer she tackled me to the floor and with her head, caressed my fur and licked my face. We play-fought until we both began panting and then just sat up. I looked back at the handsome Native American boy; his jaunty half-smile lifted the pain from my heart and eased my thoughts. The love of this boy gave me such a positive feeling.

"Elu, are you OK? What happened? We were so

worried about you." Natia communicated with me.

"It was Duane, Number 28 from UCLA. I met him the other night. It was perfect. It was special. We both had just embraced each other and then he was in pain...the sky..." I started having flashbacks to what happened.

"What? The sky what, Elu?"

"Ao-Toto." I dropped my head down.

Natia placed her head under my snout, pushing it back up and licked me.

"Whatever it is, Elu, we will get through this all together and we will be OK."

"I know, Nat. I just hope it's as simple as that. Duane's an immortal. He transformed attacking me and in my defense I retaliated, transforming too, so then he ran away."

"Elu, you had embraced him already. The bond is already formed," Natia explained.

Tate walked over and placed his hands over my fur.

"Elu Black, how about some real food?" he said.

I nodded.

"Great, you might want to go back to the other Elu. People may get a bit worried if I'm walking down the road with an oversized coyote and a wolf." He laughed.

Natia and I raced down through the forest and came across a huge boulder where we could transform back into our human forms without anyone in sight. It took me a while as it was my first time and it hurt a little with limbs bending. Natia and I met Tate back at the entrance. He was waiting inside a blue 1991 Chevrolet Silverado. It looked pretty beat up but he suited it in a nice way.

"Nice truck!" I shouted as Natia and I ran over.

"Thanks. I picked this bad boy up in a fairly cheap deal," he smirked.

"Yeah, how did you manage that then?" I replied.

"I know some people who know some people," he said, looking over his seat back at me.

I smiled and then placed my hand on his shoulder. As much as everything was majorly messed up right now, Tate had this hold over me. He could always make things seem like they would get a lot better and that's one of the connections I loved about him.

"I'm starving. Where are we going, guys?" I said, rubbing my stomach.

"I've got the perfect place," Natia said while grabbing me into her for a cuddle.

"I just hope they don't serve raw rabbit."

"Huh?" Natia frowned at me.

"Have you ever had raw rabbit, Nat?"

"No? What?" She looked confused.

"Well, I had to eat so I just hunted the most appealing thing I could back in the forest. What about you, Tate?"

"Oh." She laughed.

"Can't say I have, Elu," he said, looking into his rearview mirror at me.

We pulled up to a restaurant with a sign saying Guisados Tacos at the front. I laughed because I knew exactly what Natia was implying.

We all sat down at a table and ordered some food. I was really hungry, more than usual, so I ordered quite a bit of food. I ordered a steak picado, chiles toreados, and a big glass of orange juice. Natia and Tate got something small and just watched me scoff down my food, but I was so hungry from not feeding my human body, it just didn't matter what I ate or how I looked while eating.

"So, El, what happened to you back there? You just disappeared," Tate said.

As far as I knew, Tate was unaware of the whole Duane Toa situation and I didn't really want to break it to him because I knew how he felt about me.

"Um...I...uh...was walking to the Tommy Trojan and I just started to feel that my body was changing, so I ran through the back alleys and then I turned," I lied.

"Oh...Did anyone see you?" he replied.

"No, I just stayed in the back alleys and made my way to the forest when paths were clear."

"Tate...I, um, wanted to ask you. I'm worried for Elu about being a hybrid. Are there any immortals you know that can help Elu on that side of her heritage?" Natia asked.

With a mouthful of tacos, I paused and looked at her like, 'What on God's green earth are you doing?'

"You know?" Tate looked suspicious.

"Yeah, it didn't take a genius to know what she was. Back there at the bar, when she decided to shot-put that guy, it kind of gave it away." She laughed.

"Huh." I had no idea what she was doing.

"Yeah, I'm in contact with a family over on West Hollywood, Sunset Strip; The Hawks," Tate said.

"Why didn't you mention this before, Tate?" I snapped.

"Wow, El, chill. I was going to but you decided to turn into a coyote and disappeared for a few days."

"Oh...my bad."

"So when can we meet them?" Natia said while sipping on her drink.

"Well, it's a family. There's Cain, the father of the

family, an elderly man who didn't want to die when he found out he had cancer at the age of fifty-five. Then there's the mother Christina, who was left for dead on the desert roadside of Vegas where Cain found her and turned her before she could die, and there are two children, Eva and Cassius. Eva ran away from home. After her abusive parents were jailed in the UK, she found herself waiting a bar in Sweden. In an attempt to defend her colleague in an armed robbery, she was bitten and turned. After realizing she had become an immortal, she traveled around the world to find help for her new life, from Korea, Syria, Peru, and then here in Los Angeles where she met Cain and he took her in. And then there's Cassius. Cassius lived in the favelas of Rio de Janeiro. His mother was heavily addicted to drugs and his father was killed in a drug war. He did his best to look after his mother but after an abusive relationship with his step-father, his mother was killed, so he avenged his mother's death by shooting his step-father point-blank in his face, killing him in broad daylight in the streets of the favelas. He then went on the run as the police were looking for him. He slummed it from street to street. On his tenth birthday, he broke into a local store and stole some food. Running across the roads of Ipanema to the beach, a car hit him and the driver bit him to save his life, turning Cassius. The driver so happened to be a good friend of the family; his name is Dante Grey. He finds new breeds and places them with good families to help them and saves people from dying to give them a second chance at life. He brought Cassius to the Hawks."

"They sound like they've all had it pretty rough," I

said while finishing up my food.

"Yeah, they sure have, but they are wonderful people. They will openly help anyone who needs it and I'm sure they'd be delighted to help you, Elu. Cain knows many people all over and is well respected. He can help you," Tate said.

"That's great. When do we get to meet them?" Natia said.

"Well, I've already spoken to Cain and Christina and they're both happy to meet you guys when you're ready."

"That's cool. How's tomorrow? I'm kind of bummed right now." I slouched on the table.

"Perfect. Let's get you home anyway." Tate hugged my head into his chest.

The sky was stained with blood. As the stars came crashing down, the moon shone brightly onto the pack of wolves behind me. I ran toward the wolves for shelter, but every step I took just made the distance greater. As I stopped and looked back, the sun began to rise and overlap the moon. An urge for violence arose in my body; for anger, for blood. I tried covering my face to make it all go away but as I removed my hands from my face, blood smeared onto them and dripped from my mouth. As I wiped the blood away, I looked back up and I could see Duane; his hair was tied back and his back was to me. Then I heard him. "Elu," he said.

I cried and began walking toward him, and as I approached him, the sun completely overlapped the moon. The wolves ran away and the blazing red sun illuminated the earth a dark blood red. As I placed my hands on the back of his shoulders, I began crying. He placed his hand on top of mine to comfort me but he didn't turn around. I looked back at the sun and a silhouette of a bird flew in the not-so-far distance and as it came closer and closer, it cawed, diving straight toward us.

"Elu!" Natia said, standing over me.

I screamed and my body began to shiver and sweat.

"Elu, I'm here. It's OK. It's OK. It was just a bad dream."

It was just a dream but it all felt so real and it had to mean something. I needed to know where Duane was. My heart just couldn't bear to know that he was out there by himself. What was he feeling? What was he going through? I now knew why Natia had asked about a trustworthy immortal family. It was to see if they knew whereabouts Duane was, but Tate didn't know that. I hoped he wouldn't take it the wrong way.

"Here, drink this?" Natia handed me a cup.

"What is it, coffee?"

"Nah, water."

"Oh…" I replied disappointed.

"What was the dream about?" Natia said as she took the cup back off of me.

"It was horrible, Nat. The sky was red, the stars were falling from the sky, and the wolves…the wolves. I couldn't get to them. I tried but with every step I took they just seemed further and further away. Then the sun it, it…overtook the moon and the wolves ran away. I started to turn, Nat. I started to turn into an immortal and then Duane was there. He called me and then…and then I started crying and this bird, this big black bird…this crow…Tate…"

"Tate what, Elu?" she replied.

"Tate was the bird," I said as I tried to understand what the dream meant.

"What did he do, Elu?"

"He flew toward me and Duane. He must be the Red

Indian in Tate's dream. It all makes sense now but I can't leave Duane, I can't. I know Tate's trying to protect me but I can't, Nat. I can't leave him." As I worked it all out, my eyes moistened and tears dripped and rolled down my face. I came to the realization that Duane could be the root of all our troubles, but how could I just discard someone that I'd fallen for and that I share my soul with? If he was to die then so would I. I just didn't want to live with the eternal heartache it would leave me with. I hoped that I would be with him in this life and the afterlife.

"Wow...slow down, tiger. Don't get worked up, El. Tate will help us sort this out and we will find Duane." Natia hugged me in close and kept me there until I stopped crying.

I was a wreck, to be fair. My head was all over the place. My body was in three different dimensions and my love life was going to die before it even began, but I needed to follow through with meeting the Hawk family. If anyone knew where Duane was, it would be them, with the assistance of their friend Dante Grey.

Tate picked Natia and me up around midday. We drove down to Sunset Strip where the Hawks lived. It took about thirty minutes. On the way to the Hawks, it was pretty silent apart from the noises coming from Tate's truck, so Natia thought it would be a good idea to stick the crackling radio on and sing along to Mickey Guyton's Pretty Little Mustang. It was funny because Tate started to join in and, good lord, that boy couldn't sing; but then neither could I. It lightened up the mood, though. With all the immortals and oversized mythical animals, we sometimes forgot that we were still young adults and it was OK to have fun.

We pulled up to a white house; it was pretty old looking with stairs leading up to the front door. The house was charming. It had a garage with a massive tree at the front. As we got out of the truck and made our way up the stairs, Tate placed his arm around me.

"You have nothing to worry about, Elu. These are good people," he said.

I smiled unconvincingly and carried on walking. It wasn't them I was worried about, it was more about Duane, but screw it. I'd just take it as it came. It was only the whole of humanity relying on me. Tate knocked on the door with me and Natia on either side of him. A handsome gray-haired man answered. He was an older gentleman but you could clearly see he looked after himself.

"Come on in, don't be shy," the gentleman said.

We all stepped into the house. It was beautiful; dining room to the left, living room to the right, and big wide stairs in front of you, as you walked in.

"I'm Cain. You must be Elu, and you, young lady, must be Natia. I've heard so much about you two and what a pleasure it is to have you both here," Cain said.

"Good things, I hope," Natia joked.

"Yes, of course, angels weren't made to sin. Please, follow me this way."

Natia and I blushed a little. I mean, for an old guy, he was pretty hot but we weren't here for that. Tate stood there slightly awkward. We walked into the living room where a tall brunette lady stood up.

"Hello, I'm Christina," the friendly woman greeted us.

"Christina, this is Elu and Natia," Cain said.

"Nice to meet you, Christina. You have a lovely home," I said.

"Yeah, it's real nice," Natia added.

"Thank you. It's only clean and tidy when we have visitors. The kids tend to keep me busy cleaning up after them," Christina replied.

"Where are they anyway? Christina, call them down here," Cain said as he sat in his chair.

"EVA! CASSIUS! Can you get down here, please? We have guests," she shouted up the stairs.

"Kids…Can I get you something to drink?" Christina said as she poked her head back into the living room.

"Yeah, sure, I'll have a glass of water, please," Tate replied.

"Natia, Elu?"

"I'm OK, thank you," I replied.

"Can I trouble you for a cup of coffee?" Natia asked.

"Of course, no problem."

Tate, Natia, and I sat on the three-seater couch next to each other. Cain sat in his chair opposite us and we all just kind of sat there in silence for a minute or two.

"How is Dante, Cain?" Tate asked.

"He is well. He went away to Florida just recently to help the new breeds out there; trying to get them on the right side," he replied.

Florida...I thought of the mountain lion back in the forest. He'd told me he was here to get help from the immortals back in Florida. Maybe he'd found Dante and that's who he had been looking for.

A blond-haired girl came walking into the front room smiling. She walked over to Cain and sat on the arm of his chair. She looked no older than Natia and me.

"Eva this is Elu, Natia, and, of course, Tate, you met the other day," Cain said.

"Hey, how are you guys? Cain tells me you're a hybrid, Elu. Bet that's something," she said in her cheerful voice.

"Yeah, it's all pretty new to me." I paused.

"It's OK, Elu. I will do the best to help you. You're in good hands. Eva, where is your brother?" Cain said as he got up out of his chair and walked toward the bookshelves.

"I don't know. He was here a minute ago. I think he went over to the arcades with the Sunset Boys," she replied.

"That damn boy. I told him to stay away from them. They're bad news; hanging around the arcades all day and night," Cain snapped.

"Oh, Cain, stop worrying. Cassius is perfectly fine looking after himself. Here are your drinks," Christina said as she walked into the room and placed the drinks on the table.

"Hmm…maybe so," Cain muttered. "Right, here it is…" Cain pulled out a book from the shelves and sat back down on his seat.

We all sat there intrigued and waited for Cain to tell us about this book he was holding. Then we heard the sound of the front door opening and closing.

"MOM!" A young boy shouted.

"In here, honey," Christina replied.

"That stupid owner from the arcades tried saying that we stole…Oh um," Cassius started to say in his foreign accent as he walked in, but then looked up noticing they had guests.

"What do you say, Cassius?" Christina nudged him.

"Sorry?" he said as he put his head down.

"No, silly, introduce yourself."

"But, Mom, you just said my name," he said confused.

"Cassius Tiago Hawk! Now!" Christina said firmly.

"Come here, smart-ass, I'll introduce you," Tate said.

"Uncle Tate! I didn't see you there." Cassius ran over and sat on the arm of the sofa, next to Tate.

"This is Elu and Natia. Say hello." Tate said as he made Cassius shake our hands.

Cassius whispered something in Tate's ear and then began laughing. Tate grabbed him around his head and scuffed his hair up.

"Cassius, what have I told you about those arcades?" Cain said.

"But, Dad, it wasn't our fault—" he started to say.

"I don't want to hear it! Enough, Cassius," Cain said firmly.

"Dad…" Cassius pleaded.

"Enough. Sit there and be quiet. Uncle Tate will tell you another story about his travels if you behave."

"Stories, ay?" Natia smirked at Tate.

"So, Elu, I understand you had been feeling something similar to how new breeds do when first turning," Cain said as he put his glasses on.

"Yeah, it was at this bar, Thanksgiving Day. Tate cut his hand and it made me panic. Then the blood fell onto my hands and I just felt an urge for it," I replied.

"Yeah, that seems like any other immortal," he replied.

"Then some guy put his hand on Tate and I threw him across the bar. I wanted to hurt him but Natia stopped me and then we left."

"OK, so firstly, because you're a hybrid, you have inherited both abilities; from the transformation of a Coyote and, of course, the abilities of an immortal. You don't need blood or flesh to keep you going because your body can run on being a coyote or human, which is good, plus an increase in strength, speed, and immortality."

"Doesn't sound too bad then," I joked.

"Well, yeah, you seem to have caught the best of both worlds. But be careful not to dwell on your bloodthirsty instincts because it can overtake you if you're not careful."

"Right, I know the whole Great Coyote story and that I'm the heir, but how did I come across being a cannibal...Sorry, I mean immortal?" I said placing my drink back on the table. Everyone was deadly silent. Even Cassius seemed really interested in the conversation.

"Elu…There are always going to be answers people cannot give you. Some things you will have to work out for yourself, but if you weren't turned by an immortal then it's a question that you need to ask yourself because it becomes a bit more personal. It's something I can't give you an answer for."

I didn't understand half of what he was jibber-jabbering about but like most things, I was sure the answer to that question would come with time. I needed to ask Cain about Duane, to see if Dante could find him, but I didn't want to say anything in front of Tate.

"So other than that, it's just knowing when to control and enhance my abilities?"

"Exactly! We will help you as much as we can and you're more than welcome here anytime. The door is always open and that goes for all of you," Cain said.

"Thank you so much. It means a lot," I smiled at the sound of Cain's comforting words.

"Elu, I have faith and belief in you. We're all behind you." He smiled.

Christina stood up.

"Right. Eva, Cassius, can you help me set the table please? Dinner in five," she said as she walked out of the room.

Cassius stood up and ran into the next room. Eva

took the book from Cain and placed it back onto the bookshelf.

"Oh wow, dinner too." Natia smiled.

"Yes, of course, we wouldn't dream of sending you away on an empty stomach." Cain grinned and he left the room to help the others set the table. Natia, Tate, and I sat there looking at each other, nodding as if everything was running smoothly; but I knew why I was really here and so did Natia.

"You OK, Elu?" Tate said.

"Yeah, I'm feeling fine. Everything's falling into place." I smiled behind my lying words.

"So, Tate, how do you know the Hawks?" Natia asked as she leaned forward off the couch.

"Well, Thanksgiving night, when all that stuff happened at the bar, I made a quick exit because I didn't want things to escalate. I strolled down on to the beach staring at the stars, remembering my mother, and just trying to stay focused on her. I knew that with had happened to Elu was going to make things somewhat difficult. That's when I bumped into Dante. He was with a friend of mine, from back in Florida, who had come to visit me and my family in Kansas. His name's Iye."

I started to flashback to my time in the forest and the time I'd met Iye. Part of me had known that he knew Tate from the way he'd talked to and addressed me.

"Iye is from the Jaega tribe in Palm Beach. He is a

very trustworthy person despite the fact he has the traits of a puma." Tate looked at me as he said this. I knew he was referring back to what had happened in Pit River with the Achomawi tribe.

"So you met, Dante?" Natia asked.

"Yeah. It was a shock to see Iye all the way here in California, so after we hugged it out, he told me about the troubles his tribe was facing, in Florida, with the immortals. He introduced me to Dante, who was going to help him over there. When I asked if Dante was a part of a tribe, he told me he was an immortal, but Iye swore by him that he was a good friend and a trustworthy person. When all was said, Dante told me about the Hawks and how they wouldn't hesitate to help us."

"Wow, small world, hey?" I smiled.

"Yup, sure is," Tate replied.

"Ladies, Tate, dinner is ready. If you could follow me this way," Cain said as he guided us to the dining table.

We all sat down at the table. Cain was at the head of the table and Christina on the other side. We sat opposite Eva and Cassius. The table was laid really elegantly with lit candles, a white tablecloth, and silver cutlery; the whole works.

"You really didn't have to go to all this trouble, Christina," I said.

"Oh, this is no hassle whatsoever. You're our

guests," she replied.

Cain poured some wine into his glass and was interrupted by Eva.

"Cain…" She linked her hands into Cassius' and Cain's.

"Oh, of course. Tate, girls, you don't mind, do you?" he said as he reached his hand out to Natia.

"Oh no, of course not," Tate replied.

Cassius closed his eyes and started to say grace.

"God, thank you for blessing me with my family and new friends, Natia, Elu, and Uncle Tate. Thank you for this food and thank you for life but, please, have a word with the arcade owner…"

Christina nudged him and we all laughed.

"Sorry…God, thank you for blessing all of us. Amen." He giggled in his cute little voice.

We all mumbled "Amen" after Cassius and began eating. It was nice to have dinner with a family after so long. They were just like any other family apart from being supernatural beings. They argued like most families, they laughed and smiled like most families, and they loved each other like all families. It was a warm, comforting feeling knowing they had accepted us into their home as friends.

"So, Natia, I understand you came all the way from the paradise island of Samoa. How is it?" Cain asked.

"It's nice. You're more than welcome to come and stay with me and my tribe, anytime. It's home." She smiled.

"We will definitely be taking up that offer, Christina." He smirked.

"Hmm…" she mumbled uncomfortably.

"Christina is scared of flying." He laughed.

"No, I'm not," she snapped.

"Oh, come on, Mom." Cassius laughed.

"Only because it makes my stomach turn," she replied.

We all laughed. As we talked over dinner, told stories and joked, the night was coming to an end and I still hadn't talked to Cain about Duane. I decided to excuse myself to use the restroom and on doing so I threw my cell phone on the couch in the living room so that I had an excuse to come back later. I came back downstairs into the dining room to see everyone drinking tea and listening to Tate. I took a seat and listened in.

"So, Cassius, since you have behaved, how about the story of how I met Iye, the man your Uncle Dante is helping in Florida?" he said as Cassius paused from eating his dessert.

"Yeah!" he shouted enthusiastically.

"So, back in my village, Coldwater, some others and I were playing near the recreation park and we saw this wounded mountain lion. My friend Gabriel and I helped the mountain lion by sharing our water with it…"

"Weren't you scared that it would attack you?" Cassius asked, intrigued by what Tate was saying.

"Well, no, we just wanted to help him, Cassius. We didn't think about him attacking us. The others ran off back to the village to tell the elders, but our bravery saved the mountain lion's life that day. We made a stretcher out of our T-shirts and rucksacks and carried the wounded mountain lion back to the village. As we came close to the village, people ran out to help take the mountain lion in. When he gained consciousness we came to realize he had the ability to transform into a human, and as he did so, he was no older than Gabriel and me. He told us he'd been playing with his friends back home in Florida but had been attacked by poachers and kidnapped. When he had a chance to, he made a run for it. They were planning on killing him and a bunch of others in Colorado to sell his fur. As he made his escape he was shot, which left him wounded, but then Gabriel and I found him."

"Are you and Gabriel still friends with Iye now?" Cassius said.

"Um…yeah…Iye and I are good friends. We visit each other from time to time. He is a good person with a good heart and is very fast when racing through the woods," Tate smiled, but there was more to the story than he was telling.

"So where is Gabriel today, Uncle Tate?" Cassius asked.

"That's a story for another day, Cassius."

I could see Tate was hurt behind that smile. Something was telling me it had to do with his friend Gabriel.

"Oh…" Cassius moaned.

"Cassius, bath now please," Christina said.

"OK, Mom. Thank you, Uncle Tate. When will you come around again?" he asked as he stood from his seat.

"Um…I'll pass by soon." Tate smiled at Cassius.

"Promise?" he replied with his big innocent eyes.

"Promise. Now go bathe, you smell." Tate laughed.

"See ya!" he shouted as he ran upstairs.

"Right, I think it's about time we made a move," Tate said as he looked up at the clock on the wall.

We all stood and made our way to the front door. As we said our goodbyes, Christina and Eva gave us a hug and went off to begin clearing the table and taking leftovers and empty plates into the kitchen.

"Let me see you out," Cain said.

As we walked out, Cain laughed and teased Tate about his new truck.

"Thank you for a wonderful evening, Cain," Natia said.

"Cain, thank you so much for all your help and generosity," I said.

"Anytime, girls. My door is always open to both of you. Come by anytime," he replied.

"OK, Cain, take care and we'll see you soon." Tate gave him a hug and shook his hand.

As we left the Hawks' house, we walked down the stairs toward the truck. After Tate and Natia got in, I decided to put on my act.

"Oh shoot! I've left my phone inside."

"I'll go get it. Wait here," Tate said as he unclipped his seat belt.

"No, no, it's fine," I snapped back at him as I quickly went back up the stairs.

Cain opened the door as I knocked with his big smile and his glasses resting on top of his head.

"Forgot something, have you?" he said, but he could see the worried look on my face; my eyes filled with sorrow and tears, and the heartache of someone completely missing from my soul, as I stood before him.

"Yes, yeah come in and we'll have a look." He looked over my shoulder and held his hand up to Tate as if to say 'give us five minutes.' He closed the door and held my hand and guided me into the living room.

"Elu?" he whispered, as I moped and tried to sniff back the tears and agony engulfing my soul.

"Cain, Tate can't know," I whispered while wiping my tears away.

"What is it?"

"I know Dante is not here at the moment, but I need his help."

"Sure, Elu…" He rubbed my shoulder.

"Well, you see, I bounded with this guy. I embraced him one night with my soul and he accepted me, but out of nowhere, he began changing. His eyes turned blood red and he tried attacking me…"

Cain rushed over to his bookshelf and ran his fingertips through the books searching for the relevant literature. Someone started knocking on the door. We were running out of time. I couldn't cover all of this up if Tate was to come in and see me like this.

"Cain! Can you get that please?" Christina shouted from the kitchen.

"Yes, love! Bear with me," he shouted back.

"Here! Here it is! Elu, I know what this is...Don't...Don't worry. I will get on the phone to Dante as soon as possible. Take this book, it explains about the coming of..." Someone knocked on the door again and this time louder.

"Cain! For God's sake!" Christina shouted.

"Sorry, honey, just one sec," he shouted back.

"Oh...OK, his name's Duane Toa. He's built, about six foot three, tanned, dark long hair, and a distinctive Polynesian tattoo on his right arm," I said while Cain scribbled it down.

I could hear the door begin to open and Eva was talking to Tate. Cain forced the book into my hands.

"Hide it somewhere," he whispered. My eyes were all puffy and watery. I couldn't let Tate see me like this. He would know I'd been crying.

"Elu!" Tate shouted.

"He's coming. What do I do?" I whispered to Cain.

"Sshh...close your eyes," he whispered back.

"What?" Then out of nowhere, Cain chucked a glass of water in my face. What the hell is he doing? I thought. I turned around placing my hands on my face and wiping the water out of my eyes.

"Elu?" Tate said as he stood right before me.

"She only knocked my glass of water all over her

trying to find that damn cell phone! You kids, ay!"
Cain covered it up well.

"Huh…Oh, I'm so sorry, Cain. I didn't realize you
were there." I played on it. Cain handed me my cell
phone.

"It's fine, dear. It's only water." He laughed.

Eva and Tate stood there with looks on their faces
that read, 'What the hell?'

"Elu, you got your cell?" Tate said.

"Yeah…" I said as water dripped down my face.

"Let me get you a towel quick," Eva said she ran
into the kitchen.

We waited by the door. The book Cain gave me was
slipping from under my armpit underneath my
sweater.

"Here you go, Elu." Eva gave me a towel and I
quickly wiped my face. Tate was standing next to
me and I could feel the suspicion lurking around me.

"Right, trouble, let's go."

We finally said our goodbyes and got into the truck
and drove back to the apartment. Tate had to shoot
off so he didn't stick around. Natia had crashed out
on the bed by the time I got back from the showers.
She'd had a long day. I didn't blame her.

I wanted to read this book and see what I could find

out about this prophecy. I took my book bag and my crow caller just in case and made my way down to where it had all begun; where I had embraced my soul with Duane's, to Tommy Trojan.

As I walked out of the apartment and made my way to Tommy Trojan, I began to feel nervous about Duane coming back. As I crossed West Jefferson Blvd, I stopped and paused. It was bringing back the memory of that night. Cars passed, people passed, the stars shone through the dark sky, and my stomach was just one massive nest of butterflies. I began walking again past West 34th Street where I usually split up from Natia when we went to classes. Turning the corner on the side of Cromwell Field, my nerves began to feel stronger and stronger. I had to stop and breathe. I felt as if a panic attack was creeping up on me and I was agitated to just get to Tommy Trojan.

As I carried on walking with the statue in sight, I began to calm down as there was no one around. My heart trembled at the absence of Duane. As I looked past Alumni Park, where it had all happened, I closed my eyes to just feel what we'd once had here together. It wasn't the same. It was just a lonely feeling of a deserted soul left to suffer by itself. I sat on the edge of the water fountain with Tommy Trojan in sight. As I reached into my book bag, searching for the book Cain had given me, and passing over the crow caller, I pulled out the average-size book that was burgundy red with a gold outline on the border. The middle of the book cover had an emblem of some sort and it was called *A Prophecy of the Coming*. I opened the book. The pages were quite worn out and the ink was very faint but readable. As I turned the page, it showed the following:

Index

The Beginning

As I scrolled through the index, I came across the 'Apisi' pages, 71–80; reading that sent shivers down my body and heightened my focus on the book. I flipped the pages until I got to page 71 and I began reading through material that explained who I was.

'Apisi,' the title given to the successor of 'The Great Coyote.' The Apisi will come when the world is at the hands of the oppressors once again. As the guardian of this world, The Great Coyote helped mankind rebuild their tribes and homes after the genocide of the Red Indians. The Apisi will follow The Great Coyote in becoming a fierce leader, a great warrior, and a peacekeeper of the land, leading many tribes into battle against the evil ones. The Apisi will triumph and restore peace in the land through many ba—

Wait, I needed to know about the situation between me and Duane, I thought to myself as I stopped reading about Apisi. I turned back to the index.

The Immortals

'Curse of the Underworld,' pages 190–216. Surely that would have some answers. I flicked with my fingers through the pages to 190. I couldn't see the number on the page because it had faded from the book being so old, but the title read 'Curse of the Underworld', so that was good enough. I read through the pages; some bits seemed familiar from what I'd been told already and some just gave me more depth into what I already knew.

Upolu Island became hell on earth with the ruling of the Malietoa 'Ula. The gods couldn't let the Immortals rule and destroy the world again so the Moon Goddess cursed and banished them to the underworld. But before Malietoa 'Ula was banished, he impregnated a tribeswoman on Upolu Island who would carry his bloodline until a male was born and became of age, in order to resurrect Malietoa 'Ula and his army. The Moon Goddess knew of his plans and burdened the bloodline to only produce female relations. After a very long period of time, the bloodline would dilute and disappear forever, leaving Malietoa 'Ula and his army to remain in the underworld forever. But the clause in this situation was that a god could not harm an innocent soul; a soul of a child. The bloodline would only mate with immortals; therefore, some of the bloodline would

*stay true to the Malietoa. The Moon Goddess's
ignorance made her lose focus on Upolu Island's
occupants after centuries, as she attended to help
elsewhere, and finally, a male heir would be born.
Once he comes of age he will resurrect the Malietoa
'Ula and his army. A sky filled with blood will
symbolize the coming.*

It all started to make sense now. Duane was the
chosen one, from the Malietoa, to resurrect the
immortals, but there was nothing about me
embracing him as my partner and as the successor of
The Great Coyote. It could have been anyone in the
world, but it so happened to be the bloodline of the
Malietoa. Why couldn't it have been Tate? I thought
to myself. The more I tried to convince myself it was
a lie, the more I would inflict pain on my soul, as
Duane was the only person I wanted and needed. On
that note, I decided to call it a night and walked back
to the apartment to get some sleep.

The next day I waited anxiously for my cell phone to
ring, hoping Cain would call or Dante would get in
touch. Exams were coming up but I just had no
interest. Every day I kept thinking about Duane and
myself; about what was going to become of us, and
when the Malietoa 'Ula would arrive. I grabbed my
books and sketchpad and made my way home after
study period. I was walking down the corridor
toward the exit when I saw Jason with a big smile on
his face. I tried to put my head down and to carry on
walking past him.

"Elu!" he greeted me.

"Hey, Jason."

"How are you doing? Haven't seen you in a while."
He placed his hand on my shoulder but I slouched so
his hand would slip off.

"I'm great, thanks Jason. Just been busy." I really
wasn't in the mood to have a conversation.

"Oh…OK. Well, I'll let you get on…Oh, by the
way, I didn't see you at the game last week. We won
24–7; it was a walk over without Duane there."
Jason laughed.

"Duane?" I snapped.

"Yeah, he had some sort of problem with his
immune system; something like that. They played
awful without him."

"What? How do you know this?"

"It was in their college paper and on TV…Why?"

"Oh yeah. Yeah, of course, it was. Has anyone seen
him since?"

"Yeah, he was interviewed a couple of days after,
saying he was going to a private hospital to have a
speedy recovery. The dude looked so pale…Why
you so interested anyway, Elu?"

"I'm not. Listen, I've got to go. Catch up soon."

"Yeah, see you later…Don't forget the Victory Bell
game on the twentieth," Jason shouted back at me as

I walked off home.

As I rushed out the doors of the art campus, I reached into my bag for my cell phone. I swiped it open and rang Natia immediately.

"Come on, Nat," I said to myself as I listened to the dial tone.

"Hey, El," she answered in her cheerful voice.

"Nat, listen, I found something out. Apparently, at the UCLA game, Duane wasn't there; and he wasn't there because apparently, he's ill or something like that."

"But he's not. He's a bit more than—"

"Yeah, I know that, but listen to this. In the UCLA paper and on TV he said he was going away for a while to a 'private hospital' for a speedy recovery," I said with some excitement.

"Elu, that's great and all, but listen to me, I don't want to see you hurt. Just don't take this out of context; Duane is still in a dangerous place. Right now, we don't know if the Malietoa has him or if he's taken a bad turn or what."

"I know Nat, I know, but this is good news, surely?"

"Yeah…Yeah, it is. I'll be home in a little while. We'll go out afterward, OK? So get ready."

"OK, OK, see you in a while." I hung up the phone.

When I got home, I chucked my books on my bed and then undressed. I took a shower and then went back to my room and just lay on my bed for a bit, just thinking; thinking about Duane. I wondered if he was OK, what he was feeling, and whether he was thinking about me. The door opened.

"Elu, get ready," Nat shouted, followed by her laugh.

"Oh yeah, I am." I got up and strutted around the room, grabbing clothes to wear.

"What we doing tonight anyway?" I asked.

"Thought we'd go over to the coffee shop...open mic." Natia winked at me and I laughed.

"Yeah, for sure. Don't know what to wear though, maybe this?" I picked up a white top with blue gems on the shoulder. It was a bit fancy.

"Um...don't wear that, Elu. In fact, wear something you wouldn't mind getting wrecked," she said with her head bowed down and her eyes wondering.

"What? Are you for real?" I said as I raised my eyebrow.

"Yeah, seriously."

"Um...OK." I chucked on a really long white top, some jeans and flip-flops.

We walked down to the coffee shop, both in a really good mood. Natia had her arm around me as we hopped, skipped, and sang Mumford & Sons' *I Will Wait* down the street. As we turned into S. Figueroa Street, Tate flew down onto one of the benches on the corner.

"Well, look who it is!" Natia laughed.

"Where have you been hiding?" I asked.

Tate cawed and flapped his wings while waddling along the bench.

"Nope! Not at all! Girls' night, Tate. Sorry dude!" Natia laughed and began walking, swaying us from side to side as she carried on singing.

"Sorry Tate!" I shouted back over my shoulder at him.

We headed into the coffee shop and sat where we'd first met Tate. We were laughing and joking; it felt good to just be normal for a bit and forget about everything else.

"Nat, what are you having? I got this," I said as I stood up.

"Um…large hot chocolate," she said and smiled back at me.

"Nice, be right back." I walked over to the till and ordered two hot chocolates for Natia and me. The atmosphere was warm and mellow, so we could just relax.

"So what surprises have you got up your sleeve?" I

asked, placing the drinks on the table.

"Huh…what do you mean?" Natia giggled.

"Don't worry." I laughed.

"Hey so, Elu, apart from our crazy life and everything that comes with it, how you finding college?" she said while sipping on her drink.

"It's OK, I guess," I said as I tried hiding behind my mug.

"Elu? Come on, I know you've got exams on at the moment. Just wondering if you're balancing things well. I know it's hard with everything."

"It…It is, Nat, but I'm managing. I've got a great piece I started before I got here but it's one of those pieces of work you can't rush and you can't just give up on. It's kind of like you admire and cherish that piece of work so much you don't want to finish it because once it's finished it's over, but you know it has to be finished one day, just not today…"

The conversation went dead silent.

"Elu, you are one special being, you know that?" Natia had a big smile on her face as if she was a proud mother.

"I am?" I was slightly confused.

"You are…I don't think you realize how pure your innocence is and how sweet your soul is." She placed her hand on top of mine.

"Thank you. I don't know what I'd do without you."

A guy stood up at the mic and announced, "Ladies and Gents, a couple weeks back we had a beautiful young girl who blessed our stage with her angelic voice and she's here today to do it once again. For those of you unfamiliar, please, give a warm welcome for the wonderful Natia Kelly."

Everyone began clapping and I started cheering Natia on.

"Go get em!" I shouted to her over the clapping.

"Here we go again!" She smiled.

Natia walked toward the stage with people clapping and cheering her on.

"Thank you. I want to share this song I have been writing ever since I've been here in the States. It's a song about a girl on her journey through life remembering her ancestors. Hope you like it." She began singing with the softest, most delicate voice, which captured the audience's attention and seized the moment. Once again, I was in complete awe and amazement. The crowd paused as she finished, leaving a short moment of silence to take in and appreciate what they had just witnessed and then they began clapping and whistling. My cell phone began ringing and it was a number I was unfamiliar with, so I ran outside the coffee shop where it was quieter to answer.

"Hello?" I answered the phone.

"Hello, is that Elu?" a male voice replied.

"Yeah, who is this?"

"Dante Grey. I'm a friend of Cain's. He told me about your situation—"

I interrupted. "Yes! Dante, how are you? Any news on Duane?" I spoke too fast, trying to get answers out of him.

"I'm good, thank you, Elu. I have been in contact with Duane. I'm currently at 109 S. Carmelina Avenue in Brentwood Heights. Can you come over tonight?"

"Yeah, sure, Nat and I—"

He interrupted me. "Come alone, Elu. It's important you come by yourself. Duane isn't in a stable frame of mind."

"Is he with you?" I asked ecstatically.

"I will explain when you come over. Come alone."

"Oh...OK...Um...of course, yeah, thank you," I stuttered. I could see Nat was looking over to our table for me and then she looked around so I headed back inside.

I walked back inside toward our table. I just wanted to quickly grab my things and then let Nat know that I had to go.

"Elu, are you OK?" she asked in a worried tone.

"Yeah, I'm OK…Listen, that was Dante. I…I think he's found Duane. I've got to go…" I stuttered and rushed to grab my things.

"Oh…do you want me to come with you?" Natia replied.

"No, Nat, it's fine. I'm just going to cab it. I've got my cell just in case," I said while heading out of the doors and hailing a cab.

Natia was left in the coffee shop sitting by herself. I felt bad ditching her like this but I had to see Duane. This was something I couldn't hold off. I had to be selfish in order to get answers.

The cab pulled up outside a white-fenced house with bushes standing tall, guarding the property. I got out and walked over to the gate. As I opened it, my heart started to pulse immensely and my body started to fluster. With every step I took to the front door, my feelings became stronger. I raised my left hand to knock on the door. It was shaking uncontrollably; I knocked three times. The door opened and a broad, black-haired, East-Asian man opened the door.

"Elu?" he asked.

"Yeah…Um…Dante, right?" I stuttered.

"Yeah, nice to meet you. Come in." He opened the door wider for me to enter.

"Come through to the kitchen. I was just trying to fix this damn headlight…hence the scrappy clothes," he said while wiping his hands.

"Oh…so…um…" I was a bit confused.

"Duane, right? He's in a bit of state at the moment. I haven't seen anything like it before, really, but I know what's going on so it's all under control," he said, fiddling with the car bulbs.

"Is he—?"

"Here? Yeah, he's right under us. I've had to keep him restrained. What with him being a new breed and all, he's a bit thirsty," Dante said very sarcastically, still trying to fix his headlight.

"Dante, seriously, this isn't a joke." I started becoming angry and upset at the way Dante was treating this whole situation.

"Wow…chill. Everything will be fine. Listen, you can't go through life being serious all the time, especially when it's not the greatest of times. Sometimes you need to just relax and let it be. What's written is written and what will be, will be."

"Great…Why can't I sense him? All the past times I was around him I could feel him," I asked skeptically.

"Oh…about that; we had a problem last night," he said, scratching his head.

"Problem?" I asked worriedly.

"Yeah, I kind of had to get him unconscious for a while. He was doing so well on the animal blood but got a little grouchy last night, so I tied him up.

Remaining conscious would have been a bit
difficult," he said, turning around while rubbing his
head.

"What the hell! Tying him up? Unconscious? Take
me to him now!"

"Yeah, sure, just after I finish this. Do you want a
drink, by the way?"

"You're joking! I don't want a damn drink. I just
want to see Duane now!" I was really starting to get
pissed off.

"Ah…No can do. He won't be awake for a while
and when he does wake up, he will want to feed so
I've got a bag of animal's blood for him. He may not
be his normal self for a while, Elu."

"I don't care. I just want to see him!" I shouted.

"Thirty minutes. He'll be up in ten, and I'll feed
him, talk to him, untie him, and let him know you're
here, so he can freshen up, OK?" Dante said as he
started to put his tools away.

"Yeah, sure…Will have to wait, won't I?" I said in a
mood.

"Stick the kettle on and help yourself. I'm going to
put this away and get cleaned up." He picked his
toolbox up.

I felt slightly embarrassed and immature about the
way I'd reacted.

"Sorry, Dante, I just want to see him."

"I know, Elu…He's here now. He's in good hands."
He smiled.

I stuck the kettle on and made some tea. It wasn't
what I'd normally drink but I knew coffee would
have just made me more agitated. Thirty minutes
seemed like an eternity. I looked around Dante's
house. It seemed like a really nice family home but
as far as I knew it was just him by himself. I went
into one of the restrooms to freshen up so Duane
didn't notice how run down and worried I was about
him. As I looked in the mirror above the sink, my
eyes were puffy and my skin was pale. I looked as if
I'd been crying and hadn't slept a wink. As I reached
for the tap, my hands were shaking so much it felt
like there was an earthquake happening in the palms
of my hands. I placed my hands under the water and
let it spread along my fingers and into the center of
my hands. I then lowered my face down into the sink
and splashed the water up, but as the water collided
with my face, my heart began surging, my gravity
lost its balance and pulled me down and my body
began to rise in temperature. He was awake.

I could feel his loneliness, his anger, and his pain. I
knew everything he wanted to share before I could
even see him. Our bond was strong. Our souls
shared everything. I rushed back into the kitchen and
waited for Dante to come back up. When Dante did
come back up, he smiled and waved me over toward
the cellar door.

"He knew you were here before I even mentioned

anything," he said.

I smiled and slowly trod down the stairs. Dante left us alone to pick up where we'd left off and there he was. He was sitting down, his dark black hair rained over his face and he was topless. His tattoo started at his wrist and ended on his broad shoulders, snaking its way onto his chest. With his head down I could feel a smile sneak in on his mysterious face.

"Elu…" he said in his deep voice.

I took a step closer toward him; my body was shaking.

"It's OK. I'm OK. Dante has been helping me." He raised his head and I noticed the scratch marks on his chest from the night we first met.

"Duane…I'm…I'm sorry…" I whispered.

"Don't be sorry, Elu. It's fine. I'm good. How have you been?" He stood and walked toward me. I clutched onto the banister of the stairs.

"How are you so cool and OK about all of this?" I asked.

"Dante found me at the right time. He helped me and told me about what's going on. Some things you just have to learn to accept."

"Yeah, you're telling me…"

"What, so I don't get a hug after all that?" he snapped.

I raised my head out of confusion and then smiled looking ahead at his handsome face. I immediately ran over and wrapped my arms around his waist, burying my face into his chest for a while.

"Where did you go?" I mumbled into his chest

"I just ran. It was a lot to take in but I didn't want to hurt you so I just ran," he whispered down at me.

"I'm glad you're OK." I smiled, looking up at his face.

"I'm glad you are too." He winked.

"Let's get out of here—"

He interrupted me. "I can't…I've got to stay here until Dante says I'm stable. He said it will be another day or so. Won't be long now."

"Oh…well, I'll stick around for a bit." I smiled.

"Ah…Afraid not, Elu. Duane needs his rest. Drop by in two days and you can come pick him up yourself. We still have a lot to discuss," Dante said while walking down the stairs.

"OK, cool…Well, um…two days…" I said as I walked away, clinging onto Duane's finger.

"Two days…" Duane winked.

"I'll see you out, Elu," Dante said.

Dante walked me out and I felt a sense of ease and

comfort as I knew Duane was in good hands. My heart felt that it could cope, knowing we were going to be OK. I couldn't wait to tell Natia, but in the back of my mind, I knew I still had to get around to telling Tate, which was going to be hard.

"Elu, come back in two days and I'll have him all ready for you. Your very own vegetarian vampire." Dante laughed.

"Thank you, Dante. This means so much to me," I replied.

"Ah...No worries. He's a good egg deep down...You need a lift home?"

"Nah, I'm good, plus, I can't let you leave Duane alone. I'll catch a cab."

"Sure. Yeah, you're right. Oh, before you go, check this out!" He ran over to his car and got into the driver's seat. He turned the headlights on and off.

"Works perfectly!" he shouted.

"Yeah, great. I'll see you in two days!" I laughed, shouting back at him.

I caught a cab back to the apartment. I felt so happy and at ease that things were starting to fall into place. I rushed up past the other rooms on the way to ours to find Natia and let her know that Duane was safe and in good hands, but as I arrived onto our floor, the corridors were trashed with clothes and broken furniture. Something wasn't right. I felt an irregular pulse in my hands as if my body was warning me of a nearby danger. In the not-too-far distance, I could see our room door wide open and the light piercing from the room into the corridor. Natia would never leave the door wide open like that, so with the irregular pulse warning me and the worried feeling of something happening to Natia, I sprinted to our room and swung by the side of the door frame, into the room.

It was an absolute mess. Our beds had been flipped over, furniture had been smashed, and clothes were all over the place. Then, as I looked over everything, my heart sank at the sight of blood dripping from the window's broken glass and onto the floor. I rushed to look outside, but no one was there; just glass shattered on the floor. I swiped my finger into the pool of blood on the windowsill and sniffed it. All I could think was 'Natia.' It was hers. My coyote instincts kicked in straight away. I could smell her scent. I'd follow it. I ran out of the room and straight into Jason.

"Elu, what's going on?" he said as he held me.

"Jason, call the police. We've had a break in. I have to find Nat," I said in a rush.

"Where is she? Are you OK?"

"Just call the police! I've got to go!" I rushed off, sprinting down the stairs.

I ran outside and across West Jefferson Boulevard and when there was no one in sight, I transformed into my coyote form and sprinted through the back

alleys. Natia's scent was leading me to Santa
Monica Pier so I had to be careful. No one could see
me hiding in the shadows. I wondered where Tate
was and why he wasn't there to protect Natia. I
made my way to Tongva Park out of sight and
transformed back into my human form. Santa
Monica Pier was too crowded to be walking around
as a coyote. I made my way across Ocean Avenue
and onto Santa Monica Pier and Natia's scent was
getting stronger. She had to be around here
somewhere. That irregular pulse came back again.
This time it was on the back of my neck. I looked
around like a lost child and eventually, the scent led
me under the pier where I noticed an overly big paw
print in the sand. I kneeled down and picked the
sand up and smelled her scent. She was heading for
Canyon Park. I sprinted toward the park along the
beach and into the darkness, out of sight. When it
was safe, I transformed back into my coyote form
and dashed as fast as my four legs could take me,
cutting through the sand and gliding through the
wind. The scent was becoming stronger but with the
scent of Natia, a trail of danger lurked. Someone was
on her tail. I had to get to where she was fast.

I got to the Canyon Park out of breath and panting. I
couldn't be tired now; Natia was in trouble. I needed
to help her. I just focused on her scent and carried on
following it. After fifteen minutes in Canyon Park, I
saw what seemed to be a tall man with a red cloak
that covered half of his body, while the other side of
him was dressed in black under the cloak. As I
slowly approached closer I noticed his jet-black long
hair, a bit like Duane's, but it only covered half of
his head. The other half seemed to be covered with

dark, mysterious marks and patterns, like tattoos;
like tribal tattoos, like Polynesian tattoos…And then
it clicked.

'The Malietoa…' I said to myself and then with
every ounce of my coyote body, I rushed toward
him. My body began pulsing all over, warning me of
the danger ahead, but I shunned it off with my brave
fierce roar as I pounced right in front of this
Malietoa warrior. I stared down into his dark, blood-
red eyes. As I growled and barked to warn him off, I
could feel every single hair on my body standing up.
My tail was firm and straight, high and proud, ready
for the first attack.

The man stood before me; he stood tall and strong
with not a muscle moving. Even the great big beads
around his neck didn't move. The scent of Natia
presented itself to me again; this time from straight
under my nose. My piercing gaze left the Malietoa
warrior's eyes and wandered down to his hands that
were stained with blood; Natia's blood!

I raised my snout to the sky and howled into the dark
night under the glowing white moon. As I looked
back down, I gritted my teeth and barked at the
enemy; my eyes opened wide, and I jumped straight
onto him, going directly for his head and taking him
to the ground. He held my head in a plea to stop me
killing him but I was too strong. He knew that
sooner rather than later his head would be torn off in
utter gore for what he had done to Natia. With the
last couple of seconds he had left, he grinned
through the evilest expression I had ever witnessed
and out of his mouth came the whisper, "Apisi…"

And just like that, I consumed his head, piercing my teeth under his chin and on top of his cranium; by clenching my jaws together, I crushed his skull and separated it from the vertebrae ferociously. Just like that, the first death of a bloody war had occurred. As the head left the carcass, and I walked away from the body, it deteriorated into complete dust and returned with the wind back to the earth. Not far from where I had killed that Malietoa warrior, I could see a heavily breathing wolf lying on its side with blood dripping from a wound on its leg. I rushed forward and it was Natia.

"Nat! It's OK. I'm here...I'm here." I brushed my head into hers.

"Elu...I'll be OK, but they're here, Elu...They're looking for you."

"I know...Let's...Let's get you out of here. We need to get to Tate."

"El, I can't. My leg is in a bad way." I peeked over and she was right; she had a deep cut.

"Can you transform back, Nat? We need to get out of here."

Natia transformed back to her human form but was lying on the floor helplessly as she still remained injured.

"Nat, grab my neck. I'll carry you the rest of the way." As I sat down she grabbed onto my neck. I stood back up, dragging her body off the floor and onto my back. "Hold on, Nat. We are going to get you help." I sprinted through the woods, back onto the beach, and across the shore toward the pier.

I could feel Natia's grip slowly loosening, but I couldn't stop because people not too far away would have spotted us.

"Nat, hold on, we're almost there!"

The pier was in sight but Natia passed out from losing too much blood. The weight of her body lightened, her grip loosened, and her fingers slipped through my fur, falling...crashing into the sand. My body shook in awareness. I turned back, racing through the sand to her body. I bit into the waistline of her jeans, onto her belt, and ran the rest of the way to the pier with her body dangling from my mouth. I couldn't chance anyone seeing us but there was no way I was leaving her behind. When I got to the pier, I placed Natia down and transformed back into my human form. I rushed back over to Nat and held on to her. As I placed her head into my lap, I reached into my pocket for my cell phone and dialed 911.

"I need an ambulance. I'm under Santa Monica Pier...My friend, she's badly hurt. Please, come quickly."

I sat in the sand with Natia's head resting on my lap. As we waited for the ambulance to come, I brushed my hands through Natia's hair, trying to hold back my tears at the sight of my friend in a serious condition.

"Nat, I'm so sorry...so sorry...I should have been there for you." I sobbed.

When the ambulance came, they carried her on a stretcher and placed an oxygen mask over her face. I went with them to the hospital, but once we got there I had to stay in the waiting room until they told me what was going on.

"Miss Black," the doctor said as he came in.

"Is she going to be OK?" I asked.

"She's going to be fine. She just needs plenty of rest."

"Can I see her?"

"Unfortunately, Miss Kelly needs a lot of rest. We may release her tomorrow. Why don't you come back in the morning?"

"I think I'm just going to stick around." I didn't want to leave Natia by herself after the attack. I was scared for anyone that was close to me. What if the Malietoa were planning to hurt everyone close to me in order to get to me? What if they had already gotten to Tate?

There was no way I was going to leave Natia by herself, so I stayed in the waiting room and got comfortable. I got up and walked over to the coffee machine. As I waited for the cup to fill up, a gentle hand was placed on my shoulder. I turned around and there he was, standing before me in complete sorrow and distress. He knew the danger was upon us. He knew he had let his friends down. He knew he was meant to be a protector but he had failed.

"Where were you?" I punched into his chest. "We needed you!" I punched again and began crying. "Natia is hurt and they're here!" I cried, falling into his chest. He placed his arms around me and held me tight. His head fell on top of mine and I could hear him weep and feel his tears roll onto my face. I pulled away looking into his teary eyes.

"Elu, I'm so sorry. I didn't mean for this to happen. I was sorting things out with Cain and then this happened and—"

"Shh…it's OK, Tate. She's going to be OK," I interrupted.

We both sat down and held each other close. This was a hard time for both of us because we had grown to become so close with Natia. We didn't want to see her hurt.

"Elu…" Tate whispered.

"Yeah, Tate?" I whispered back.

"Why don't you get some rest and I'll wake you up if the doctors come out and say anything?"

"Yeah, sure…" I said as I dozed off.

"Darkness, darkness, light, light, the seeking, the searching, in chaos, in chaos…" A voice echoed through the mountains, along the stream and crept over my shoulder and into my ear.

"Who's there?" I shouted back.

"Apisi…" the voice echoed again.

"Who's there? Where are you?" I shouted.

I began walking toward the mumbling whispers, along the stream and toward the waterfall. Something wasn't right. All the fish in the water had begun swimming away from the waterfall, but as they swam past my feet, their fins cut into my skin, causing me to bleed. It was bearable but painful. I had my mind set on finding the owner of that voice. I carried on walking toward the waterfall in front of me. I could see an enormous blackbird on a branch of a tree that looked straight into the center of the waterfall, cawing and flapping at what was before it. I looked closer and to my surprise, it was a man tied up from arm to arm by the vines of the forest. With his head bowed down, I couldn't see who it was and I stepped closer toward him. The bird kept cawing, trying to warn me off but my curiosity was too overwhelming.

"You shouldn't be here," he said. I recognized the voice.

"Why shouldn't I be here? Why are you tied up and was that you calling me?" I replied. I placed my hand on his chin to raise his head.

"Don't do that! Go away now!" he shouted at me. The bird flew down on the man's shoulder and cawed at me yet again, trying to warn me off, but this time he pecked at me to leave this man alone.

"You need help. Who are you? Do I know you?" I began backing off.

"You know me but you don't know us. We know all about you." His voice began to change as if he was being possessed and something began to take him over.

"What!" I frowned in confusion.

The man raised his head with his hair streaming down his face. His eyes were glowing red and thick; dark blood trickled down his chin and onto his chest, as he looked deep into my soul. The horror was right before me as I looked straight back at the monster that was Duane.

"Duane?" I said in terror.

"No...We've come and we will get our vengeance, Apisi!" he screamed.

The black bird cawed louder and louder as it began pecking down at Duane's skull, piercing his skin, and causing him to cut and bleed from his forehead. The bird cawed again and again as if it was telling me to run. I stepped back but the cuts on my feet made me fall into the water. As I fell into the water that was slowly turning red from my blood, the vines began to release Duane and his arms ripped through the clutches holding him back. He grabbed the bird

around the neck and off his shoulder. Right in front
of my eyes, he clenched the bird's wing and tore it
off its body. He chucked it aside like a rag doll. He
then made his way to me with the most hideous, evil
grin on his face. He fell to his knees in the water that
had become filled with my blood; then, as he raised
his hands toward me, I screamed.

"Elu!" Tate shouted. "It's OK. It was just a bad
dream," he added.

"What…I…Duane? Where's Duane?" I said with
my eyes pacing back and forth and my heart racing.

"Duane?" Tate replied.

"Miss Black, she's up bright and early. If you would
like to follow me, I can show you where she is," the
doctor said as he came in.

Tate looked at me, knowing I wasn't telling him
something. He knew there was something wrong but
didn't persist, as he knew this wasn't the time or
place. We followed the doctor to Natia's room and
there she was, sitting up, looking out of the window.

"Nat!" I shouted as I ran over to her.

I gave her a big hug, but as I pulled away I could see
her eyes were all puffy and red from crying.

"Nat, it's going to be OK. He's gone forever and
Tate and I are here."

Natia looked over at Tate and then I looked over at
him with suspicion. He put his head down and

walked over to the window.

"Well?" I said. "Is someone going to say something?"

"How long have you got, Natia?" Tate said staring out the window.

"The doctor said I have to wait till they discharge me, but my leg will be healed by tonight," she said with no emotion.

"By tonight? Nat, are you crazy!" I frowned.

"Elu, it doesn't take me long to recover," Natia said.

"Right, we need to go as soon as you're ready," Tate said.

"Go where? Why aren't either of you making sense?" I replied, looking back and forth between them.

Tate turned back around and walked to the end of the bed where I was. He sat and leaned over right into my face.

"Elu, listen to me. At this point we need to make sure we are all prepared for things that are going to happen. We cannot put our guard down for anyone. This is life and death, so get your shit together now!" Tate snapped at me.

I was shocked that Tate would speak to me like that; I guess we were all agitated about the situation.

"Tate..." Natia frowned.

"No! Elu, stop acting like a child. You have responsibilities, now stop chasing some fake love story and focus on your destiny!" Tate said aggressively.

The room went dead silent. I'd never heard or seen Tate like this. He clearly knew about Duane and he wasn't happy. I hadn't wanted him to find out like this but it was all said now.

"Tate...I—"

"Elu, save it for another time. We have more important things to concentrate on right now, OK?" he replied.

Tate grabbed Natia's belongings.

"I'll wait in the car. Don't be too long," he said.

As he left, I looked at Natia, trying not to cry as I could feel the intensity fill the room and the bitter words that had stunned me speechless.

"Oh, El, come here," Natia said, lifting her arms and inviting me for a hug.

I hugged her tight. I didn't moan or make any noise. My facial expression didn't change at all, but tears crawled down my face from my eyes as I felt the guilt and sorrow in my body for not being straight with Tate.

"It wasn't meant to be like this, Nat," I said.

"It was meant to be anything you want it to be, Elu. Prophecy or no prophecy, you control your destiny, not Tate, not me, not the Malietoa, and not Duane," she replied.

She was right. We got the release papers from the doctors in the end and made our way to Tate's truck. Nat had to be on crutches just until tonight.

"Where are we going?" I asked.

"I'm dropping you two off at Cain's and I need to inform Red Bear and the Achomawi tribe. I'll be back in the morning," he said looking dead ahead at the road.

"Tate, you can't leave, it's not safe," I said.

"No, Elu. He's right. The people need to know, to be safe, that the Malietoa are here," Natia said.

"Are you just going to ignore me?" I said while looking straight at Tate.

No answer.

"Tate!" I shouted.

"I will talk to you when I'm ready, your highness!" he said with cockiness.

"Great…" I mumbled.

We arrived outside Cain's house and we all got off the truck. Tate helped Natia up the stairs and I rang the doorbell. Before I knew it, Eva had opened the door.

"Come in, guys. Everyone's in the front room," she whispered.

"Oh, hey. Oh, OK," I said.

I walked into the front room. Everyone was there. Cain sat on his chair with Christina on the arm next to him. Cassius was sitting on the floor reading a book, and, surprisingly, Dante sat on the sofa.

"Sit down guys," Cain said.

"Dante, what are you doing here?" I said.

"Oh, hey, we haven't met yet. I'm Dante," he said as put his hand out to Natia.

"Oh, hi… ignore the crutches. I'll be off them in a couple of hours," she replied.

"Immortal?" Dante smiled.

"Wolf," Natia replied.

"Crow," Tate interrupted.

"Hey! Chogan! How's it going dude?" Dante greeted him.

"Yeah, not too great at the moment. Listen, we'll catch up soon. I need to get down to Pit River," Tate said.

"Yeah, no worries. I'll see you soon," Dante stood

and shook Tate's hand firmly.

"Cain," Tate nodded. Cain nodded back and he took his leave.

"Dante! What the hell are you doing here? Where's—?" I was interrupted by a voice coming into the room.

"Hey, stalker."

My heart immediately raced to a fast pace and I got up and ran over to this six-foot-three giant and tackled into his chest for a big hug.

"Duane!" I said.

"Seriously, Elu, he's all yours now. Whatever he gets up to is between you and him. Don't come to me anymore. You're both just as crazy as each other," Dante said.

"What? I thought you weren't stable for another day?" I said.

"He isn't, but after Stretch Armstrong here started bench pressing my equipment and curling the water dispenser, I had to get him out of there. Plus, if he makes one bad move his head will be a trophy in my game room." Dante laughed.

"Yeah right, you and what army, dwarf?" Dante laughed.

"Guys, sit down. We need to speak," Cain interrupted.

"Sure." I sat down next to Natia.

"Budge up, champ," Duane said to Cassius as he picked him up and put him on his lap.

Cain started speaking and then Natia whispered to me.

"Hubba, hubba."

I giggled like a schoolgirl.

"Ladies…please," Cain said.

Duane looked over and laughed.

"Sorry," we both muttered.

"Right, Tate's made his way to Pit River to let the Achomawi tribe know we need—" Cain said but then was interrupted.

"Who's Tate?" Duane said.

'Shit!' I thought to myself. How do I explain Tate to Duane.

"He's one of our good friends, Duane," Natia said.

"Sorry, and you are?" Duane replied.

"Natia Kelly."

"Guys, come on now, stay on the subject. There will plenty of time to get to know each other properly later. We need to stay focused right now, OK?" Cain said.

"So what are the plans then, old man?" Dante said.

"Well, we now know the Malietoa are here after the attack on Natia—"

"Damn, are you OK? I'm still finding it hard to believe I have the same blood as these scumbags," Duane said.

"I'm fine. It's OK. Elu dealt with him anyway," Natia replied.

"What do you mean?" Duane said.

"Well, she killed him…" Natia replied

"Really?" Duane looked shocked and then smiled at me. "Badass!" he added and then winked at me.

"Natia, how did this all come about with Malietoa?" Cain said.

"Well, I was back in our room tidying up and the other students must have been getting ready to go out 'cause I could just hear loud music and shouting; nothing out of the norm. I then heard a knock on the door so I stopped what I was doing and open the door, but there was no one there; just loud music and the football players shouting from their rooms. After I pushed the door shut, I carried on doing what I was doing but this smell of awareness just lurked around the room and started to become more and more intense. I turned back around to the door suddenly; no one was there but the door was slightly open so I walked toward it to close it shut. As I placed my hand on the handle, the door flung open and I was on my ass. The Malietoa was standing over me; he was wearing all-black and a red cloak that covered one side of his body, with these great big beads that hung around his neck. He clutched onto my neck and lifted me off the ground while squeezing my throat. I fought back, clawing at his arms. As I started to transform, he whispered, "Apisi" through his dark evil smile and chucked me through our bedroom window. Before I hit the ground, I transformed into my wolf form and sprinted off to Canyon Park." Natia picked up her drink and sipped on it before carrying on.

"Did he say anything else to you?" Cain said.

"When I thought I'd finally lost him, I tried to calm myself down and find a place out of sight, but the sense of danger stayed creeping at every direction, so I had to stay on guard. Before I knew it, there he was again, standing right in front of me. As I backed up, I roared and growled at him but he was just too strong and quick for me. After I had caught some glass in my leg, he said to me, 'Don't run, child.'

'What do you want from me?'

'Where is Apisi?'

'What do you want with her?'

'Her?'"

"I paused because I realized that I had given him information that he hadn't known."

"How did you know where to find me?"

"Malietoa 'Ula knows…"

"Where is he?"

"You'll soon see, Masina Nu'u."

"Then he grabbed me by my throat once again and slammed me onto the floor, damaging my leg even more. But then, when I thought that he was going to kill me, he stopped…It was like he knew you were coming; he felt it. He flung me aside and waited…Waited for you, Elu."

I already knew all this but when Natia put it across like that, and with all these people here sitting next to me, I realized we were going to war—a war that had started centuries ago— and I was going to end this evil conquest once and for all. No one else was going to be hurt by these people, I swore to myself.

"Elu," Duane called.

"It's OK. I know what's coming and I know you're all here because of me. It means a lot to know that even when my back's against the wall, I still have all of you. I won't let you down. Tate's taught me so much, Natia's given me so much strength to become what I've been prophesied to be, and Duane, well, we haven't spent much time together but it will all be worth it once this blows over," I said.

"We're all here for you, Elu," Christina said.

"So this is what we're going to do: Christina, Cassius, and Eva, you're going to fly over to Montana and stay with the Blackfoot over there—"

Cain said before being interrupted.

"The Blackfoot are still around?" I asked.

"Yes, they are Elu," Cain replied.

"But…But why didn't Tate tell me?" I asked skeptically.

"It doesn't matter right now. We need to stay focused," Dante said.

"Natia, once you're healed up you'll go with Dante to Canyon Park. We need to make sure they stay out of the way of the public so no innocent people get hurt."

"Got it, Pops," Dante said.

"What about me?" Duane said.

"Duane, you and Elu are going to stay together. You'll be stronger together. I want you both to keep your guard up. Stay hidden in the woods until Tate creates a diversion," explained Cain.

"But he's with the Achomawi," I replied.

"He'll be back and with help, I'm sure of it."

"Dad, what about you?" Cassius blurted out.

"I'll be OK, Cass. I will stay with Uncle Tate," Cain replied.

As everyone began to get ready, I stayed seated on the sofa. With so much racing through my mind, the only person I wanted to see and talk to was my dad. He gave me hope on my worst days and today wasn't going to be so great. I headed out back and made the call while the others were preparing for the battle.

"Hello?" the person said on the other side of the phone.

"Dad?" I replied.

"Elu?" the person replied.

"Hey! Uncle Yancy, how are you? Is Dad about?" I asked.

"What's up, El? Yeah, one sec…'J! Elu is on the phone!' He's coming now. You OK?"

"Yeah, I'm fine, Uncle Yancy. Just wanted a quick word with Dad. How's everyone back home?"

"Yeah, we're all great thanks El. Come home soon. We all miss you."

"Will do…"

The phone scuffed.

"Elu?"

"Dad? Dad, can you hear me?" I replied.

"Yeah, El, I can hear you. Are you OK?"

"Yeah Dad, I'm OK. I guess I'm just feeling a bit down. I miss home and stuff." I couldn't tell him what was really going on.

"Head up, El. We're all so proud of you. You can come home anytime you want. The whole tribe misses you."

"I know, Dad. I miss you all too. Just tough being out here when you're all so far away right now, but I don't want to give up."

"Hey! What have I always taught you? Winners never quit…"

"Quitters never win…Thanks, Dad."

"That's my girl! Go get them! Anyway, I got to run. Your Uncle Yancy and I are going down to the lake to do a bit of fishing; you know, Grandpa Tyee's birthday and all…"

"Oh Dad, I'm so sorry, I forgot all about it…I've been so busy with college and that, I forgot all about Grandpa Tyee's birthday."

"It's fine, Elu, really. I know how busy you are."

"Dad, can you take some flowers from the garden to Grandpa Tyee's tonight for me?"

"Of course, I will. Listen, El, I better go before your mom finds me talking to you and then she's going to chew my ear off."

"OK, Dad, love you." I laughed.

"Love you too, princess." The phone cut off.

When I was younger, I'd pick flowers from our garden and take them over to Grandpa Tyee's house every Sunday. Then when he passed, I still brought flowers over to his house but only on his birthday. Grandpa Tyee was special to me. He always used to tell me stories about brave tribesmen, especially after dinner on Sundays. He sometimes talked about my grandmother. I'd never met her, but she was one lucky lady to have Grandpa Tyee. I often remember when Grandpa Tyee used to catch me being naughty or not doing my homework. He would tell me about the 'Basket Ogress,' a cannibal lady who kidnapped naughty children and put them in her giant basket and then ate them later on. Grandpa Tyee always said, you have to be on top of your homework and stay smart because the Basket Ogress was dim witted and could be easily out-smarted if you were clever enough. It makes sense now; she was an immortal.

"El?" Duane said as he poked his head out the back door.

"Oh hey," I replied.

"Everything OK?"

"Yeah…Yeah, just a little spooked."

"Don't worry, I won't let anyone or anything hurt you. I'll be right there."

"I know." I walked over toward Duane and placed my fingers into his hand.

"You two, in the front room," Cain said swiftly as he passed the back door.

Duane and I walked back into the front room. Everyone was standing up and ready to make a move.

"What's going on?" Duane said as we entered the room.

"The Malietoa have been spotted by our friends in Nevada," Eva said.

"What? Where?" I replied.

"Outside Vegas. We need to move quickly," Cain replied.

"Change of plan. We're not going to let them come to us. We're going to bring the fight to them. We're going stand tall and wait for them at Death Valley," Cain added.

"How cliché." Dante laughed.

"What? Why there?" I replied.

"They won't expect it Elu. If they know where we are because of me, it will be better to go to them. It will confuse them and I don't want anyone else getting hurt in this crossfire, so somewhere more deserted will be better," Duane said.

"What about Tate?" I said unconvinced.

"Already on it. Eva, make your way down to Pit

River. Catch up with Tate and let him know the news. As soon as you're done, go and stay with the Achomawi. I don't want you to be anywhere near this when it happens," Cain said.

"But, Cain—" Eva said before being interrupted.

"No buts! Just do it!" Cain snapped.

"Right, Dante and Natia, same as before, you two stick together. When they come, you two will be the first to engage," Cain said as he started to pack some things into a bag.

"Christina, take Cassius and leave for Montana now. Let the Blackfoot know that Apisi is here. Look for the tribal leader. His name's Mingan."

Christina kissed Cain and left holding Cassius's hand.

"OK, now, you two stay hidden. No matter what happens, you don't move until Tate arrives," Cain said to me and Duane. He went on talking about the game plan.

It was about 8 pm and Natia's leg was all healed. Everyone was ready to leave. Christina, Cassius and Eva had already left long before us. I just hoped Tate would make it in time before the Malietoa came. As I looked out of the window at the big bright moon, I felt a strong presence tower over me.

"Don't be scared, El," Duane said.

"I'm not scared. I'm just a bit unprepared," I replied.

"Unprepared? El, you're the chosen one, you are the ONE," Duane said firmly.

"No, I'm prepared for this battle…I'm just not prepared to lose any of you," I said as I turned around, looking at Duane. He raised my head up by the chin with his thick fingers.

"Hey! You're not losing any of us. Just as you're prepared to fight, we are going to bring the fight too." Duane smiled.

I wasn't convinced, but I couldn't let that cloud my emotions. Right now I needed to stay focused. We headed out toward Death Valley where we would wait for Tate and the Malietoa to join us. Natia and Dante drove up together and Duane and I went up with Cain. The ride up was so intense and uncomfortable. Everyone was feeling the anxiety. The nervousness and the adrenaline pumping through my body were so noticeable on my face. Not only that, but Duane and I shared emotions, so he felt it too.

"Elu, it's going to be fine. Just try and focus on something positive to fight for," Duane said as he looked over his shoulder and into the backseat, where I was.

I nodded and smiled as I exhaled. He was right. I needed to concentrate on something that was going to make me push through this. So, deep down in my mind, I dug as far as I could and thought of everything that was going to get me through all of this. The first was my parents and my family. I

couldn't just die. No, really, I couldn't just be killed
because who would explain to my mom, my dad and
my family that their only child was killed by ancient
Polynesian cannibals resurrected from the
underworld by their heir; who so happened to be the
person my soul unconditionally bonded with. I
couldn't let Tate and Natia down. I'd become so
close with these two very special people, that I owed
it to them not to be killed, and to protect them. Then
I thought about Duane and how I felt when I
couldn't be with him when I needed to be. How he
must have shared the same feelings. I couldn't let
him feel like that for the rest of his life, regardless of
the situation at hand and the length of time I'd
known him for. The whole world, the whole galaxy,
and the universe had literally pulled me to this one
person and made me fall madly in love with him,
bringing me to this point. Now I knew exactly what
love meant. It meant to be with someone who, even
though you try to keep your mind off your heart, will
still remind you. It meant you'd never want to see
that person hurt or in danger and that you would
always want what was best for that person, even if it
meant putting them before yourself.

But this was deeper than my personal feelings; this
was for all the tribes, this was for all of mankind,
and this was for my ancestors. Right then, I felt the
fire in my belly, the blood rushing through my veins,
and my fingers curled into my palms, clenching into
a fist. I squeezed my eyelids shut and I felt the urge
and aggression rise through my body, but it didn't
burst through. I maintained it and harnessed the
feelings under my control. As I peeled my eyes
open, I felt my senses as a wolf, felt my urges as an

immortal, but I remained in my human body. Everything was under my control. Duane quickly turned to look back at me, as he must have felt what I had just done.

"El, you OK?" he asked, worried.

"Good God!" Cain shouted as he looked into the rearview mirror at me.

"What! What is it?" I started looking up and down at my body to see if it had changed, but it hadn't.

"Your eyes…" Duane said.

I leaned forward into the front seats and looked into the rearview mirror. My eyes had changed but like I'd never seen before. When I'd changed into my coyote form, my eyes would turn white and when my immortal instincts had kicked in at the bar, my eyes had turned red, but this time my eyes had turned white with a red outline around the iris.

"Oh shit, what does that mean?" I said looking into the mirror.

"Sit back for a sec and let me look at you properly," Duane said.

"Elu, you're a hybrid. You've controlled both sides," Cain said.

"Oh…badass," I whispered to myself. Duane smiled and winked at me as he began nodding; he was impressed.

"Elu Black, the heir to The Great Coyote, the first Native Hybrid," Cain addressed me. It only fueled my focus and concentration more.

We pulled over onto the dirt, off the road, and parked in the middle of nowhere as if someone had just dumped their car.

"OK, we're here," Cain said.

"Those mountains are a bit of a distance from here," Duane said.

"Really?" Cain replied as he looked to me.

"Huh?" I was confused. The mountains were far from here. Why didn't he drive closer?

"Oh, not you too. For goodness sake, you're an immortal, use your legs, and you, Elu, you should be able to get up there in a flash," Cain said as he opened the door and got out of the car.

"Oh yeah…still not used to that," Duane said.

I got out of the car and closed the door. Duane grabbed my hand and pulled me into him.

"Elu, I won't let any harm come to you. We're all ready and we're all here for you," he said.

I looked up into his sturdy silver eyes as they began to dilute into the venomous red, immortal transformation.

"Duane, your eyes; they're turning," I said.

"I know…I got this." He smirked. He bowed his head down closer to mine and the tip of his nose touched the arch of mine. I placed my hands on the side of his face and drew my lips closer to his.

"I got you." I pressed my lips to his and kissed him. I felt so secure in his arms. It gave me a feeling of hope and clarity.

The car boot slammed.

"You kids ready or what?" Cain said. Duane released his lips from mine and raised his head back up, grinning at Cain.

"Waiting on you, Pops!" he shouted.

"Let's warm these muscles up and then first one to the peak?" I said.

"Ready when you are, El," Duane replied.

"Let's do it," Cain added.

"On your marks, get set…GO!" I shouted.

Off we went. Before the dirt rose from the ground, the following step had already landed. We raced through the desert to the mountains. Duane was really fast and so was Cain, but I wasn't even trying and I had taken the lead. Looking back over my shoulder, I could see Cain's intense face as he battled Duane for second place. Duane was smiling, trying to catch up, but he was no match for me. The wind whispered past my ears and caressed my body softly, moving me swiftly along. I punched into the mountains with my body shaking and trembling down to its foundations. As I climbed to the finish line I jumped and clung onto the limbs of the mountains as the clouds rose out of reach. I waited at the peak of the mountain for Cain and Duane. I raised my nose to the sky and howled and screamed declaring my win; my battle cry, and my call to the gods.

"Almost had you, El," Duane said.

"You wish," I replied.

"Looking good, Elu. Can't wait to see what you can really do," Cain said.

"Where are the others?" Duane said.

"El!" Natia shouted.

"For an ambush, you guys are really loud," Dante said.

"Hey, Nat!" I replied as I ran over to hug her.

"El, your eyes?" Nat said.

"I know. Don't worry. It's good…" I replied.

"We've found an opening down the middle of the mountain where Duane and Elu can wait behind some rocks until the time is right," Dante said.

"That's good. You two go with Dante. I'm going to head north of the outskirt to signal Tate. You'll be safe for now; go," Cain said.

We headed down the side of the mountain and onto a
flat level where we remained hidden behind tall
rocky walls. Natia and Dante were guarding us with
their lives. Nat turned into her wolf form and Dante
was on his guard, ready for the Malietoa to arrive.
Duane and I stayed leaning behind the tall rocks.
The moon illuminated the side of Duane's face and
at just the right angle his deep red eyes absorbed the
light. The stars were brighter than usual. They were
all watching through the dark sky. I was their center
of focus and they all kept me in sight.

"Elu, you good?" Duane whispered. I snapped out of
my daydream.

"Yeah, I'm good," I replied.

"Good. Stay focused," he said.

We waited and waited for something to happen or
someone to show; every hour, every minute, every
second was becoming more intense. I kept asking
Natia telepathically if she could see anything. She
kept giving me the same answer until I didn't bother
asking anymore and instead I found a crack in the
rock that helped me see toward Natia and Dante.

"Elu, if I can feel the presence of your eyes behind
me, imagine what the Malietoa will feel looking
directly at you," Dante said, so that idea was shot
down straight away.

"Just focus and stay patient. Everything will happen
in time," Duane whispered to me.

I suddenly felt a turn in my stomach as if something

was alive in me. A scent, a smell, was making me feel like this. I looked at Duane and the expression on his face was raw anger. As his face creased and his jaw tightened, the veins in his face pulsed through and surfaced on his skin. The rock we were leaning on developed five holes where Duane's fingers were digging in and turning the stone into dust and rubble.

"They're…they're here," he gritted and whispered through his teeth.

"They're here but…but there's only five of them," Natia said to me. I could hear the growling from Natia, the knuckles crunching from Dante, and then the concrete footsteps of the Malietoa; I listened closely.

"What do you want?" Dante shouted.

"Toto…" a deep voice whispered. Natia barked and growled. My senses were so focused and sensitive that I could hear the drool from Natia's mouth drip and spurt onto the ground.

"Duane…" I whispered.

"Don't…talk…" he quietly snapped back.

"El! They know!" Natia said.

"Stay here and do not move!" Duane said. He jumped over the tall rocks right behind Natia and Duane. I peeked through the crack in the rocks.

"Ah…Tamaitiiti," The leader of the five Malietoa

said.

"I am not your child! Or Malietoa 'Ula's!" Duane shouted in his deep voice. The beast in him echoed through his voice. He stood firm and strong between Natia and Dante, with his fist clenched and his veins pumping through his arms. He was ready to fight.

The leader of the five stepped forward. He had a Mohican hairstyle. He was the shortest of the five but he was very built. His tattoos covered his neck and came up to his chin, under his nose, and paved through his face, over his eye, and through to the top of his head. He wore the same big beads as the Malietoa that had attacked Natia and also had the same attire with the dark red cloak that covered one side of his body.

"Malietoa Toa…You belong with us, Brother. Lead us under Malietoa 'Ula. These animals do not belong alongside the Malietoa," the leader of the five said.

Duane stepped forward, towering over the leader. He placed his hand on his shoulder and said, "Malietoa Toa?" He looked back past Natia and Dante to the crack in the rock where my eyes were visible as I watched over. His eyes reflected the moonlight into my sight; from that moment, I knew that even if Duane was an immortal, there was no way he'd give up on me.

Duane placed his other hand on the leader's shoulder, turned back to him, and shouted, "SCREW YOU!" as he planted his size-twelve feet into the leader's stomach and sent him crashing back into the other four Malietoa.

Natia and Dante rushed to Duane's side. My heart
started pulsing rapidly and my hands were carving
holes in the rock. The leader of the five stood up and
chucked his cloak off his shoulder.

"I WILL NEVER BE A MALIETOA!" Duane
yelled.

"You fool!" the leader of the five replied.

We were outnumbered. Where was Tate? I couldn't
stay here and not do anything. Cain said it himself;
Duane and I were stronger together.

The Malietoa made the next move. The leader went
straight for Duane, throwing a sequence of punches
as Duane slipped, ducked, and dodged all but the last
punch, which sent him colliding with the rock I hid
behind.

"Ooff!" Duane panted as the wind was knocked out
of him. I could feel all that was going through his
body mentally and physically.

"Duane…I need to be out there with you," I
screamed through the crack in the rock.

"NO! Stay put, Elu!" he shouted before running off
toward the leader to continue the exchange.

Natia took on two of the Malietoa; a very tall, bald-
headed bloke and another man who had his long hair
tied in a bun-type style and also had a very
distinctive tattoo on his chest and lower abdominals,

which became visible as he removed his cloak. She pounced on the Malietoa with the tattoos and locked her teeth onto his shoulder. As he tried to pull his arm out, the taller Malietoa made his way to Natia but she pulled and swung him into the taller one.

Dante also had two Malietoa to fight off but he seemed to be doing just fine. As he used his speed and agility to land fast punches and kicks, shattering the bodies of the Malietoa, he also fought a tall one just like the one Natia was fighting. Dante landed a right body shot followed by a right uppercut to the chin, sending the tall Malietoa to the ground. The short-haired Malietoa who fought with Dante tried to wrestle him to the ground but Dante reversed the Malietoa's hold and took him to the ground, twisting his arm into an awkward position and breaking the bones in his arm as he forced it out of place. The Malietoa retreated, all beaten up and hurt. Duane stood at the forefront of the battle with Natia and Dante at his side. I could feel the smirk he had on his face when they retreated.

"What's the matter? All that time in the underworld made you a bit rusty?" Duane said.

The leader of the five Malietoa laughed with a profound, savage, unholy laughter as the other four stood behind him in utter silence.

"Lelei...Now we begin!" he said under his evil laugh.

Duane looked at Natia as she was panting with her tongue out and clearly out of breath. She nodded at

him. He looked to Dante. His shoulders were going
up and down from his heavy breathing and he also
nodded at Duane. Duane slanted his head in a
'Whatever,' attitude and said, "Another ass
whooping? I don't mind."

I couldn't bear to see them go through this again and
again; I needed to do something. Where in the hell
were Tate and Cain? They should be here by now.
Dusk was slowly approaching as the sky started to
change color. Duane sprinted to the leader and
tackled him to the ground. As he gained top position
of the leader he began to ground-and-pound on him
but it was no use. As Duane was missing him and
punching holes into the ground, the leader flung
Duane off of him and laughed. Natia went to attack
the two Malietoa that she had previously fought. As
she jumped on the topless Polynesian warrior with
her mouth wide open to consume his head, he caught
either side of her snout with each hand. As he stared
down into her mouth, the taller Malietoa grabbed her
around her stomach and chucked her into the tall
rocks that were protecting me, and smashed her skull
into the wall, leaving her unconscious.

"Nat! Nat! Wake up, Nat!" I pleaded with her.

We were slowly getting beaten and I couldn't just
hide here and see my friends be killed. The two
Malietoa who were fighting Natia split up. The taller
one went for Dante, who was already fighting off
two Malietoa. He'd seemed to be managing fine
until the third came and then he started getting
caught by punches as they began to hold him down.
The three of them began striking him on the ground.

Duane rushed over and tackled one of the taller ones
to the ground. On the way down he grabbed the
Malietoa's head and began to twist it but the leader
of the five kept on Duane's back and pushed him
off. The other Malietoa, who had been fighting
Natia; the one with the tattoos on his chest, went
back over to her, intent on finishing her off. As he
stood over her, my animalistic instincts kicked in
and I growled at the warrior. My eyes pierced
through the crack in the rock and struck fear into
him. At first, he froze and as I growled louder he
began to steadily step back. Duane and Dante were
really struggling. I couldn't stay here anymore. I
clawed my fingers into either side of the crack in the
rock and began to tear them apart from each other.
As the tall block began to crack and crumble, the sky
greeted my ears with the cawing of a crow. I
instantly stopped and looked behind me in time to
see the watchful guardian glide down over me.
Toward the battlefield, two tall, built men were
climbing rapidly on either side of the mountain. I
had noticed them before. They were Achomawi
tribesmen. Pahana was the tall, very light-skinned
young man climbing on the left, and Nowtaku was
the other young man, climbing on the right side of
the mountain. I remembered him being quite loud
when we went to visit the Achomawi. They rushed
up the mountain to the battlefield where they both
ran toward the taller Malietoa and tackled them to
the floor. Natia was still unconscious.

"Chogan…Better late than never, ay!" Dante
shouted over to the giant crow spiraling down to the
ground. As he landed, his wings spread out and Tate
changed into his human form.

"Only five?" Tate shouted as he rushed over to the topless Malietoa. Duane came crashing down on his back from a blow the leader of the five had landed.

"And you guys are?" Duane said. Tate dodged, ducked, and avoided the attacking Malietoa.

"I'm Tate, and the two boys with me are Pahana and Nowtaku. We're here to help." Tate replied while gripping onto the wrist of the enemy and pulling his arm over his body into a judo throw.

"Cool, five-on-five. It's a fair game now!" Duane shouted as he hopped back to his feet and back into fighting distance with the leader of the five.

"Duane, where's, Elu? You need to be with her!" Tate shouted back as he began throwing punches.

"She's fine. Don't worry about me, chump; I got this!" Duane shouted back sweeping the leader off his feet and landing a devastating knee to his cranium before he hit the ground.

The five Malietoa seemed to not be letting any cracks show but we were keeping strong pressure and resistance on them. I felt helpless just watching. I wanted to fight. I was ready to fight. Hell, I could probably end this a lot sooner than they could, but I couldn't risk them seeing me because one mistake and Malietoa 'Ula would have me and the world at his feet. I walked to the end of the wall and peeped around the corner. Pahana was the closest to me, fighting with the tall Malietoa. He fought and attacked from his human form and in and out of his bear form, turning into a silver gray beast with white streaks on his fur. Natia was in sight. I wanted to get her out of danger. As I put my foot down to sneak toward her, someone grabbed my shoulder and pulled me back behind the rock.

"What are you doing?" Cain whispered.

"Cain!" I shouted as I hugged him tightly.

"Stop shouting," he whispered.

"Oh yeah…They seemed to be doing OK out there but Natia's hurt. She's just against the rock on the other side. Can you go get her? She's in danger," I said to him.

"Yes. Wait here, Elu; you can't be seen," he replied and off he went. He brought Natia behind the rocks with us. She'd be safe here. I tried waking her up but it was of no use; she was out cold.

"Elu, stay put with Natia. I'm going to take higher ground just in case the odds go against us," he said.

"OK, be careful," I replied.

I looked back through the crack in the wall. It was fifty-fifty. Tate had control of his fight. He landed a double jab, right hand with a spinning elbow that left the Malietoa on his knees before Tate. Tate then placed his palm under the enemy's chin and on the back of his head, yanking the skull off the shoulders. As it ripped off, coal-black dust oozed out of the body and soon the whole being deteriorated onto the ground, slipping through Tate's fingers.

Pahana was getting the best of one of the taller
Malietoa, taking his opponent to the floor and
turning into his fierce bear form, striking at the evil
oppressor. Dante and the short-haired Malietoa were
fighting back and forth. He was thrown into the side
of the mountain wall where he was unable to defend
the warrior's swift kick to the jaw, followed by
another to the lower abdomen; causing his body to
take the impact and sending cracks into the wall of
the mountain. Before his opponent could land the
third kick, Dante swung the Malietoa into the wall to
take his position as he followed up with a six-hit
combo to the face and to the body, making the wall
shake and produce dust from the power and speed.

Nowtaku seemed to be losing his cool. As he was
thrown to the ground repeatedly, he began to roar
and lose his temper, swinging and charging at the
second of the taller Malietoa. Before he knew it, the
Polynesian warrior cut Nowtaku deeply on his
shoulder, leaving him to defend with only one arm.
As he roared in pain, Pahana paused from striking to
look at his tribal brother in need of help and was
side-blinded by the Malietoa.

Duane was really struggling but he was relentless in
his attack. His body was catching up to him as I
could feel the pain running through it. The leader did
not slacken one bit as he out-struck, out-wrestled,
and out-fought Duane altogether. He wouldn't give
in though, as he knew that as well as his life, all of
ours were at stake too; one-two, left hook, right to
the body, left low kick, right knee all blocked and
countered by a right uppercut that dropped Duane to
his knees. As he fell, I fell to my knees too. I

searched up the wall with my hands and pulled myself to the crack where I looked through. The leader of the five grabbed Duane around the neck.

"You fought well, Toa. It's a shame I have to tell Malietoa 'Ula you decided you didn't want to join your family," the leader said.

"D...Du...Duane..." I screeched. I was too weak. Everything he was feeling was going through my body too.

This was it. This was the end. All we had gone through, all the pain, all the suffering, and searching, to lead us to this very moment. I began flashing back to my parents, that kiss goodbye, that flight to L.A., the drawing of Tate, opening my dorm room door to see Natia...but as I searched deep into my soul, the beast in me did not give up. My senses intensified, my eyes became wide open, and a furnace of heat rose up from my body. The leader paused and looked up. In front of him, he saw my eyes illuminating through the crack in the tall rocks.

"Apisi..." he whispered under his hideous evil grin.

I began tearing apart the rock from either side of the crack. As the foundation began to shatter and tremble before me, the crack began to widen, revealing myself before the Malietoa. The Malietoa tightened his grip around Duane's neck. Duane raised his hands up, clutching onto the hands of the leader to resist but he had nothing left in him to give, and then...a gigantic crow came diving down toward the leader's head. As he flapped at him and pecked at his skull, the leader released Duane. His body flopped and crashed to the ground. My eyes began flashing before me. I had seen this happen somewhere before. I looked around me as if this was all a dream. Everything seemed to be in slow motion. I could hear the crunching and chomping of Pahana's jaw on the head of the tall Malietoa as he killed him. I could hear the sweat drip from Dante's face as he bopped his head under the kick coming from his opponent, and I could hear the stomping of Nowtaku as he ran toward the second of the taller Malietoa. I looked back round to the crow attacking the leader of the five and realized this was what had happened in my dream…

"TATE, NO!" I screamed. It was too late. The leader picked the crow off from his back and with his hand clutched onto the wing, tearing and breaking it. The crow cawed in utter pain as the leader threw it to the side like a rag doll. Tate transformed back into his human form holding onto his arm as he groaned in pain.

I ran at speed toward the leader. With every step I took, every heartbeat, and every breath, my body began to shake more and more. I knew this feeling from before but this was so much stronger and more powerful than previously. My body structure broke out and became free, forming into my coyote shape. My pelt pierced my skin, shooting through, and my tail extended from my spine as it stood firmly; the sign of attack. I leaped at the leader with my enormous paws and vicious roar. The leader turned toward me as I pounced at him. We squared off and he stood there in a cocky manner before beginning to clap and laugh.

"So you have come to play?" He smirked.

I growled like never before. This was the end for him, as he was soon to find out.

"I MALIU!" he shouted and sprinted across the battlefield toward me.

We circled off. As I began to wave my tail as a distraction tactic, he tried to step in to reach me, but every time he did so I would bite and snatch and cause him to step back. As the fight became more heated and intense, it turned into a chess game; every move counted but I was too strong, too fast, and far more intelligent than this ancient Polynesian warrior. With a sharp movement, I dropped my head low and plunged at his ankle, clamping my razor-sharp teeth into him. I pulled and dragged him down and across the floor. As I let go, he tried to get up, but as he began to stand, I rammed my head into his stomach and charged him into the wall of the mountain, leaving him fatally winded. I noticed Cain above us so I backpedaled away from that area. The leader looked surprised at my sudden retreat. Pahana and Nowtaku had killed the second of the taller Malietoa. Duane was unconscious with his face planted into the ground. Tate was in agony as he held his broken arm helplessly. Natia was starting to gain consciousness but was still incapable of fighting, and Dante was still fighting one of the last two remaining Malietoa.

"You fool, you should have killed me while you had

the chance to," the leader said. His apparel barely clothed him as it hung off his body, all torn and destroyed from fighting.

I let my back legs fold as my tail lounged on the ground. I bowed my head down to my chest and inhaled through my long snout. My ears remained pointed and alert. Then, raising my head to the sky as far back as I could possibly go, I exhaled and howled into the golden red sunrise as it broke through the sky, sending my final cry to the gods, to the Malietoa, and to my friends. This was a message to say, 'I control my destiny and I am the Native Hybrid.'

My body was pumped, my blood was raging, and my eyes were flaring; this was it. Pahana and Nowtaku saw to Natia, helping her up onto her feet as she transformed back. Dante was finally winning over the short-haired Malietoa as he held him in a rear-naked chokehold. Tate began to get to his feet and shuffled toward Duane. Duane palmed his hands out to the floor. He began to stand.

The leader tore his clothing off his torso as he sprinted toward me. The fury in my eyes blazed as I darted toward him. He swung a wild, wide-open punch, which I swiftly slipped and capitalized on, clamping my sharp teeth and large jaws onto his neck, and pounded his helpless body into the wall. He clawed at my face, but with every movement he made, I sunk my teeth in deeper and deeper until I could slowly hear the air squeeze through his crushed windpipe. He held my snout with the remaining strength he had left to finally gasp his final words out of his mouth.

"Righteous or evil, you will never save everyone...my Apisi...Malietoa To..." his last words croaked from his mouth as death stared into his eyes.

I bit down through his neck, detaching his skull from his body. As the dark dust took its final form over the once-great warrior, his beads departed from his neck and fell to the floor, along with the ashes. I turned my back away from this miserable rubble and faced my alliance. I transformed into my human form and walked over to Natia, which was where everyone was standing, apart from Dante. Looking upon my friends, who'd taken some serious damage and had been left hurt and beaten from the battle, I nodded to them to say it was over. I then turned my attention toward Dante and the short-haired Malietoa.

"Elu!" Duane shouted.

"I know. Don't worry, Duane, I got this," I said as I walked toward the last Malietoa.

Dante stepped aside from the last Malietoa who was barely standing. He was hunched back, panting loudly and heavily, and with his clothing ripped and torn from head to toe. I walked straight into the face of the remaining rival and stared deep into his eyes right down into the core of his soul. In a high-speed movement, I cuffed my hand around his throat and lifted him off the ground.

"The lucky one…" I smirked.

He choked and gagged from the tightness of my grip.

"You go run and tell Malietoa 'Ula that I am here and if he wants to suffer the same fate as your comrades then let the hunting begin!" I chucked him to the floor.

He stumbled to his feet and before he disappeared he said, "You have no idea what you have started, Apisi…You will all be damned to AFI!"

I growled loudly and as it shook his soul, it sent him running off. It was done. We were all OK…For now. I turned round to my friends. The hybrid powers surged away as danger left us on this rocky mountain beyond the rising sun.

"Let's go home." I smiled in relief. Pahana and Nowtaku each had one of Natia's arms around their shoulders, helping her up; Dante held Tate up. Looking past his hair that drooped down over his face, and behind the pain he was bearing, he constructed his half-smile for me. And Duane, my Duane; my unconditional other-half, my immortal Polynesian warrior, my embracement, stood at the forefront of my new family. As the sun finally rose, it glared onto Duane; he stepped forward toward me and placed his hands on my waist.

"My native hybrid, my beautiful partner, my Elu." Tilting his head forward, we locked lips, kissing and embracing. We were totally lost in the moment.

"Pops, you can come down now!" Dante shouted at Cain.

We all laughed.

After making our way down from the mountains and leaving Death Valley, we all went back to Cain's house where we washed up, changed, and refueled our bodies.

"What on earth is that?" Natia said to Duane.

"Ah, see what we have here, pretty wolf, is a smoothie," Duane replied.

"But not just any smoothie," Dante added.

"Yeah, you don't say." Natia laughed.

"Ah but I do say. This is a nutritional 500 ml of deer's blood with ten ounces of deer meat. Why waste the meat when it's full of protein?" Duane said as he sipped on his thick red deer smoothie.

"I think I'm actually going to throw up," Natia said in disgust.

"Hey! Don't knock it till you try it," Dante laughed.

"Yeah, I'll pass…" she said.

"Squirrels and rabbits more your thing?" Duane replied.

"Just don't let Cain catch you guys. I don't think he'll be too happy with the blood bath you're making in his kitchen," I said.

"Think it's more Christina you need to watch out for." Natia laughed.

I walked out of the kitchen and toward the living room where I saw Pahana and Nowtaku carrying two large rucksacks.

"Pahana, Nowtaku, where are you guys going?" I said.

"We need to get back to our families, Elu," Nowtaku replied.

"We need to make sure the Achomawi people are safe," Pahana added.

"Oh, so soon?" I said in disappointment.

"I'm afraid so," Pahana said as he stepped forward and placed both of his hands on my face.

"Go in peace, Apisi." He took his leave.

Nowtaku stepped forward and said, "You'll be fine, Elu." He then placed both of his hands on my face and said, "Control the beast." He winked at me, following Pahana's lead.

As I walked into the front room, Tate was looking out of the front window and watching the boys leave. I crept up on him.

"How's the arm, dude," I said.

"Hey, yeah, not bad," he hesitantly replied.

We stood there silently in awkwardness.

"Listen, Tate, about Duane..." I said before being

interrupted.

"Elu…We're friends and we'll forever be friends."
He hid his emotions behind a fake smile I knew too
well.

"Right…OK, yeah, sure, friends." I smiled back.
"What now?" I added.

"Well, the Malietoa will be back and in greater
numbers. We have to train, prepare, and be on our
guard because this is far from over," he said as he
bowed his head down in fear.

"Hey, we won the battle; we can take this war." I
picked his head up by his chin.

"Schoolyard fight; the battle will come, Elu, and the
war. I don't even want to think about that right
now." Tate turned his head away from me and made
his way to the back garden leaving me slightly
confused.

"These damn cell phones!" Cain shouted tapping his
cell phone screen.

"What's up?" I said as I sat down on the sofa next to
him.

"Christina keeps ringing me but there's no reception
on this damn thing," Cain replied.

'KNOCK, KNOCK, KNOCK!' Someone was
banging on the door. It was probably Nowtaku and
Pahana. They'd most likely forgotten something.

"Elu, can you get that for me? It's Eva. She was on her way home," Cain said as he was playing about with his cell.

"Eva is coming home?" I asked.

"Mmhmm," he mumbled, more interested in his phone.

I walked over to the door and opened it but it wasn't Eva. A big figure stood in the doorway. As I looked up at the tall man with white-grayish hair, a goatee, slanted eyes, and sharp eyebrows, I was lost for words, as I hadn't expected it.

"Elu Black?" he said in his deep strong voice.

I stepped back, leaving the door wide open with this stranger standing before me.

"Who...Who are you?" I stuttered.

"I am Mingan. I am the former leader of the Blackfoot Indians in Montana," he said with a smile that left me confused.

"Former?" I asked in confusion.

"Your tribe is waiting for you, Apisi," he said.

AUTHOR'S NOTE

In 2013 I decided to start writing; after injuring my knee severally in MMA training I was out of physical activities for nine months. Rather than beating myself up about this, I hopped down to my local library and much to my surprise at twenty-two years-of-age my library membership ran out eleven years prior to me coming in. I renewed my membership and began looking for books on Native American culture, history, and mythology.

I was always fascinated by Native American culture but I began thinking how mainstream outlets shed very little light on this group of people, so I began writing.

Soon enough writing became my escapism; I was off down the local coffee shop where I would spend my 9-5 writing (*perks of working part-time*). As I began to gain momentum with the story, I wanted to see how Native American mythology would correlate with that of others like Polynesian mythology.

Writing from a female's perspective was difficult but through research, feedback, and observation I feel I successfully portrayed Elu to the best of my abilities. Elu represents strong, independent, creative leaders that I see in so many women in my life, and she will forever live on in all women of the world that stand strong with their faith, heritage and culture.

ACKNOWLEDGEMENTS

All praise to the most high.

I honestly from the bottom of my heart want to immensely thank every single person that went out of their way to purchase my book with their hard earned money. Every single reader that has experienced my novel; that in its self is a huge accomplishment for me.

I want to thank the *Native American* people for educating and giving me the amazing idea to write this book, I am ever so grateful for your culture.

The super-cool people of *Polynesia* for a loving and joyful culture that makes you one of the most loved people in the world.

To the courageous *USC Trojans & The University of Southern California,* Thank you for giving me an insight into the history and the fictional student life. *Fight on!*

My brother *Adam Taie* for doing an amazing job on all the artwork in this book, the visuals stayed true to the story and represents it in the way I imagined. Thank you.

To my beautiful wife *Sarah,* Thank you for putting up with me through this whole process and supporting me to achieve this dream, you are my world; I love you.

My father *Abdul-Rashid Patel,* thank you for encouraging my creative writing and listening to my long-winded ideas on the way to work.

And lastly but importantly thank you to my brother *Cameron Parker, Cam* thank you for always believing in me especially when no one else would this success would not have been accomplished without you. Thank you.

NATIVOS

Junto al fuego
y también junto al agua
a veces en la oscuridad
a veces en la luz
cantan
con la tierra como Hermana
con la tierra como úníca
verdad
ahí
siempre mirando
la inmensidad
con asombro
pero sin temor
ellos también
hacen humanidad…

NATIVES

Next to the fire
& also next to the water,
sometimes in the darkness,
sometimes in the light,
they sing.
With the earth as a sister,
with the earth as the only
truth.
There
always looking at
the immensity
with amazement,
but without fear
they also
make humanity…

by

Victoria Ponce
13th September 2018
The street poet from Alhambra, Spain.

'I want my creativity to expand beyond my expectations; I want every wild, far-fetched and exaggerated idea to come to fruition and exceed. Creativity lives in a open world.'

FOLLOW ME & KEEP UP TO DATE WITH MY LATEST WORK.

www.abdulahadpatel.com

38258607R00154

Printed in Poland
by Amazon Fulfillment
Poland Sp. z o.o., Wrocław